20.9.13



Tiinalle,

***Fine-Tuning Hanna***

Mukavia lukuhetkiä!

Tiina

This novel is entirely a work of fiction.
The names, characters and incidents portrayed in it are the work of the author's imagination. Any resemblance to actual persons, living or dead, or events, is entirely coincidental.



ISBN-13: 978-1492152941

ISBN-10: 1492152943

***Fine-Tuning Hanna***

## *Chapter 1*

Hanna Suvanto felt every one of her 30 years on this morning of the day-after-the-party. Actually, she thought, she felt the years of her neighbouring 90-year-old granny, and possibly the combined years of the rest of the terrace she lived in. She was now officially ancient and ready to die.

Her Nokia erupted with a 70s Finnish country tune, the singer shouting forcefully to the beat to spell out the word 'darling', *R-A-K-A-S*. On any normal day, this would have got a smile out of her, but alas, this was not any normal day. End-of-the-world did not find the bouncy two-beat of the *humppa*, a romp of a dance, even a tad amusing. Nope.

'Somebody make it go away,' she groaned. The two brain cells still operational were failing to compute that the noise related to someone wanting to talk to Hanna. After several agonising rounds, she realised that she in fact had the power to end the racket. She jabbed at her phone, and the noise stopped.

'*Haloo*?' grunted Hanna.

'Good afternoon, Queen Hanna! Is Your Highness ready to breakfast?' chirped an irrepressibly perky voice, clearly audible even though the handset wasn't anywhere near Hanna's ears. Her best friend Micheál must have anticipated this state of affairs in the Queen's household, as he was shrieking mightily at the other end.

Hanna was still residing in an entirely different time-space dimension, where everything hurt and worked in slow motion. Her hand reached for the Nokia, and sluggishly brought it up closer to her ear.

'Micheál, what the hell are you doing? Go away. I want to die alone!' All this took enormous effort to get out, from first drawing in a breath and then pushing the air back out through an incredibly sore throat and sawdust mouth.

'Darling, it is time to get back to the land of the living and the thriving. The quicker you get rid of your little hangover, the sooner you'll remember to thank me for the most fabulous party ever! You do, ah, *remember* the party, don't you?'

'I hate you, and I will never forgive you,' Hanna managed to spit out. Even though she had no spit left in her mouth.

'That's what they all say. You'll come around – and if you don't, I do have it all on tape. I can easily put the worst bits of it on YouTube – perhaps your gratitude will show up after all, hmmm? Really, darling, you were truly going for the kill last night! I've known you for ages and I have *never* seen you behave like that. "Desperado" comes to mind: it was as if you actually did think your youth was over, and you had to cram in as much experience as possible before it was too late. Have you no shame, girl?'

'Well, it's all over now. I'm officially old, and I'll never do anything interesting in my life. And by the way, I'm quitting drinking now as well: I swear it, and you are my witness. I may as well, there's no more fun to experience,' groaned Hanna, a bit of life creeping back into her voice.

'Yes, yes, that's what they all say. Hold onto your boots, I'll be around in a tick to serve my hangover-cure brekkie, so put some clothes on you, will you? Make yourself decent, etcetera, etcetera.' Micheál hung up.

'I have clothes on... oh, you're gone,' Hanna replied to the beep. 'But I *will* stop drinking now for life,' she continued to mutter to herself.

*Micheál.*

Hanna could feel a painful grimace pulling at the corners of her mouth. Fuzzy images from the night before were returning to her sore brain. Micheál had pulled off the best 30th party ever. His little "I own an event management company and I'll show you how it's done" act had delivered the goods. She could hear one of his MC jokes coming back to her – a joke that showed he had been paying close attention to her constant ramblings about her native land.

'When do you know you've been hanging around a Finn for too long?'

Micheál paused, hearing the audience come up with their best suggestions, from being too money-conscious to feeling inferior to the Swedes.

'Guys, guys, you are all so wrong!' Micheál stopped for dramatic effect. 'The answer is: when you think *silence is fun*, of course!'

The audience in the Dublin pub had loved it, especially all the Finns, who had then progressed to quietly showing the Irish how drinking was *really* done.

Micheál really was the best, Hanna thought, the smile on her face hurting a little bit less, the muscles in her face getting used to the stretched position.

More images from last night floated in and out of focus. The party had been perfect, at least the bits she could remember. Another wonderful night to reminisce about when she moved back to Finland.

Hanna opened her eyes. It hurt. It was time to get out of bed. Knowing the way Micheál drove his car – energetically, just the way he accomplished everything else in life – he'd be arriving at her house very soon. She had to make herself a bit more presentable before he showed up. There were limits beyond which even Micheál's adoring attention would not stretch – and poor after-party personal hygiene was likely to be one of them. Time to hit the shower.

*

Micheál bounded through the door like an overenthusiastic puppy, and immediately set out to create his magical hangover cure drink. It tasted disgusting but it worked miracles – Hanna began to come around to the idea of continuing her life. She could now sit up at the kitchen table, quite unaided. Progress.

Michaél moved around Hanna's kitchen, cooking a mighty Irish breakfast, the perfect mother hen. He had done this on so many occasions during the past year and a half of Hanna's life in Ireland that she'd lost count. He was just so much better at all things kitchen, and Hanna was happy to leave it to him as often as possible.

'Now, Hanna, since you are old and never going to drink again, you'll need something to fill your empty life. Did you ever hear about Sebastian O'Reilly, the Irish personal development guru? The one off the telly?' Michaél pointed at Hanna with the spatula he was using to stir the scrambled eggs, eyeballing her reaction. Hanna's face had shown no recognition of the name. 'He's starting his fabulous seminars in Dublin again, and we are *so* going. You've become way too negative for my liking lately. We need to re-install a bit of positive attitude.'

'*Mitä*?' groaned Hanna, rolling her eyes, which turned out to be a bad idea, as she felt a piercing pain throbbing behind them.

Time to be a perfect statue again, the way only a Finn could be. Stillness hurt less.

'Never mind your "mitha", missy. It is not polite to say "what?" in that tone, and you know that – even if you make it sound more exciting by using a foreign language to do it.'

Micheál looked so stern that Hanna would have burst out laughing, if she'd been able to handle the pain associated with such activity. Self-preservation kicked in before she could do anything so foolish. Stoicism was good. 'Not some phony positive-thinking malarkey, that's the last thing I need,' Hanna whined. 'If I'm grumpy, putting a fake smile on my face is not going to change that. I don't want to be sucked into one of these cults, where you hand over all your money and your passport. What would *äiti* – Mum – say if I was never able to go back to see her again?'

'Quit your whinging, girl. You are really starting to show your age – and that's the last thing we need! Where is the beautiful, young and carefree Hanna I fell in love with, when you were just off the boat, all sparkly-eyed and bushy-tailed with enthusiasm?' Micheál dramatically waved some mysterious kitchen gadget that Hanna didn't even know she owned for emphasis.

'For your information, I never got here by boat; I flew, like every other sensible modern person. Do I really have to go to his poxy seminar?'

'You do, little madam: he is one gorgeous hetero guy, and you need to settle down and have babies soon – let's not forget your age – and he is just perfect for you! I took one look at him, and I could just feel it. Well, actually I did look twice – he is a hunk. Unfortunately not for me, though.'

'What, are you my matchmaker now? I'd heard that it was an ancient Irish occupation but I didn't think you had it in you!' Hanna's frown was back. 'And by the way – I'm the only one allowed to say I'm old, nobody else. It's a bit of a sensitive subject.'

*She is seriously grumpy today*, Micheál thought. *But she'll come around*. He knew his breakfast had superpowers. 'Chillax, baby, it's all right. You are just a spring chicken, etcetera, etcetera, and I don't want any man stealing you away from what we have together.'

'We are almost perfect for each other, aren't we? I'll never forget the first time I saw you coming down the escalator at the back of St. Stephen's Green shopping centre – I couldn't take my eyes off you. It's hard to believe that's only a year and a bit ago: I feel like I've known you forever.'

'Ah, well it's me charm, you know! Mind you, I think my hair style has improved a lot since then. It was just a phase...'

'It has, darling Micheál! I don't think the whole punk-rock style suited you – I much prefer this tidy pretty-boy thing you have going on now. Your black hair, so dramatic – and I particularly love your 30s-style side parting. You are *so* good looking, you know.' Hanna was warming to her topic.

'Hanna, don't make me blush!' Micheál looked extremely pleased. 'Eat your breakfast!'

'Don't worry,' Hanna munched away. Micheál had planted a plateful of his delicious breakfast in front of her and it tasted heavenly. 'I'll eat every bit of it.'

After a few minutes' contented silence, Micheál piped up: 'It was a shame your parents couldn't make it to the party.'

'It wouldn't have really been their scene.' Hanna pierced a slice of grilled tomato with her fork and popped it into her mouth. 'Besides, Mum and Dad are on their usual trek up to Lapland to see the relatives in their campervan just now, so the timetable clashed badly. You know, I always used to have my birthday party in Lapland, in the house of one of my relatives. My birthday inconveniently fell during the summer holidays and I could never invite any of my friends because of our regular trip up there. Then again, I did always have a lot of my mad Lapland cousins at the party – so it wasn't so bad, really. And *äiti* always made sure to bake the cake. So in a way, I'm used to never having my birthday party at home. The only constant feature is the cake.'

'And you baked the best cake ever. It was delish!' Micheál smacked his lips.

‘Thanks,’ Hanna beamed. ‘But seriously – thank you for everything you did to make this party great, I really appreciate it.’ Hanna was feeling mellow, tired but good with a full belly. ‘And you know I love you.’

‘I love you, too, Hanna. But I still think we need to find you a nice little toyboy to look after you. Hmm – come to think of it, I’d like one for myself, too...’

‘You are just so bad,’ Hanna scolded him. ‘Will you ever stop harassing me about men? You are the only one I need in my life, thank you very much. Who else could look after me as well as you?’

‘Well, I’m touched, darling, but you know it’s not true – not for the long term, anyhow.’

‘I don’t need complications in my life. You are my perfect man, I have the perfect job in the concert hall tuning my lovely pianos, and that is all is there is to it. And I’m going back to Finland soon. So please give up, already!’

‘Keep your hair on, Hanna,’ laughed Micheál. ‘And I’m very contented with my life with you, too. And let’s not discuss the topic of you leaving me – I can’t face it just yet.’ Micheál’s face dropped.

‘Anyway,’ Hanna swiftly changed the subject, ‘when is this seminar on, then?’

'This Tuesday, in the Fitzwilliam Hotel on St. Stephen's Green – and we *are* going – I won't take no for an answer. I've been dead impressed by this guy for quite some time, and it'll be great to hear him live. Just recently I saw an interview with him talking about how he got into the whole personal development thing – it was really interesting. He sure has a way with words. And the way he moves, like a dancer. They were showing clips of him on stage... a fine thing! Anyway, he used to work in the financial sector in London, and he was doing really well, working the system, etcetera, etcetera. But then it started to bother him that the more he learned about it, the less sense it made to him. I think he got pretty disillusioned. All his life, he said, he'd had this great need to understand how everything works. Once he started asking questions about the financial system, he didn't feel like stopping there. He got involved in some positive-thinking seminars, asked more questions, and was so pleased with the answers he was getting that he just got totally swept away with it all. I'd really like to hear more of what he has to say. I'd say there'll be quite a crowd attending. But don't worry – I've already booked the tickets online.'

'Great,' said Hanna, without enthusiasm. 'Just what I wanted to hear.'

'Now, now, watch the attitude. When you get grumpy, you go all Nordic – so dark you're almost scary. Cheer up! We'll take the Luas light rail, shall we? I'll come over after work on Tuesday – I need to make sure you don't chicken out.'

'Ok, whatever,' sighed Hanna, 'but I'm not going again if I don't like it.'

*

Hanna was sitting motionless in the packed conference room, feeling grumpy, her arms and legs crossed tightly. She didn't want to be there, but Micheál had been true to his word, and had marched her from her house to the Luas stop in double-quick time, in order "not to be late", as he informed her in clipped tones when she whined about the speed. She could still feel that she wasn't fully recovered from the party, and the last thing she wanted right now was to try to be all bright and breezy.

In her mind's eye she could picture an event like one of those American religious meetings, where everyone got the shakes and excitedly screamed mumbo-jumbo, arms extended towards the skies. She felt embarrassed for those people already: the poor things didn't realise how badly they came across to all rational and sensible human beings. She was *so* not in the mood.

'Relax, Hanna, and smile! It won't kill you!' Micheál was bouncing up and down in his seat in high excitement, turning around from side to side to take in everything.

'Yeah, right.' Hanna felt even grumpier. In front of her, she could see smiling people chatting animatedly, which made her feel even more annoyed. She couldn't wait for the thing to be over.

A stick-thin, well-groomed lady stepped up to the platform and started to speak in a highly-polished best-of-British accent, introducing the speaker, doing the hard sell on Sebastian O'Reilly's amazing work to date. Micheál was drinking in every word, while Hanna rolled her eyes. Micheál started clapping in hyper mode when the girl enthusiastically announced Sebastian.

Then Hanna's eyes landed on the godlike creature gracefully springing up the steps to the stage. Her jaw dropped. What a… *beautiful* man. He began talking, and his voice was like velvet, caressing her ears. Being in a hearing profession, she was always very conscious of how a person's voice sounded, and this voice was like no other. Hanna let out an involuntary sigh of pleasure and settled into her seat to listen. The longer she listened, the better it got. His words were as beautiful as the voice.

'Hello, and good evening to you all. My name is Sebastian O'Reilly, and I thank you for coming out this evening. I have been looking forward to this for quite some time now. "Personal development" is the name of the game, but I'd like to rephrase that for you here tonight. It's not about trying to achieve anything or to be "better": it is a journey of highly enjoyable, neverending self-discovery. Perfection is the most boring thing of all, and truly not possible, as it means “the end”. Let’s discuss how to discover some of our hidden guiding principles. After all, the most interesting topic for us is ourselves.

‘I’d like to tell you a little bit about myself first. I became fascinated with personal development many years ago. At the time, I had an undefined urge to change the direction of my life: I was constantly looking for something, but I didn’t know what. I questioned everything. Like so many Irish people, I went to work in the UK after college. I worked in London, in financial services in the City, for many years, and my life was hectic.

‘I was always looking for the next thrill, the next big thing that would give me a great buzz. Yet I never felt properly satisfied – there was always something missing. Although I was doing really well financially, I didn’t truly understand what I was getting paid for. I started to question the financial system, and rapidly became disillusioned with it all.

‘Then one day I came across a seminar on “How to Make Money”. At the time, I was asking a lot of questions about money and what it really is, so I went along to hear more. I thought it was going to be about financial strategies, which obviously I was already very familiar with.

‘I was very surprised when the speaker began to talk about giving away money to make more. Now, that sounded absolutely crazy. How was that supposed to work? I thought *charity* was about giving money away. He talked about the 'Law of Attraction', encouraging us to take his word for it and just to believe that it worked.

'I thought he was completely nuts. I would have walked out of the room, but as I was sitting in the middle of a tightly-packed audience, it was easier just to stay sitting down and hope he'd finish up quickly. The speaker moved on to finding one's true passion in life. He asked a very simple question about earning money – one which I couldn't answer. He asked: what was the reason – what was the *passion* for me to go out there and earn?

'He asked us: Why?

'He told us to think about it for a minute, to contemplate: why did *I* need to earn a lot of money? And I realised, sitting and sweating in that airless conference room, that I had no idea. I had always thought that earning lots of money was the reason in itself, but on that day, I began to understand that it was not.

'What I learned that day was that the thing that I had been missing was my *true passion in life*. We create our world from *inside out*, not outside in. Our creation from *inside out* happens through our belief-systems, which are the definitions of our world, the filter system of our reality. There is no meaning attached to anything happening around us, except the one that we give it...'

*Wow.*

That was the only word Hanna had to describe what she was experiencing. She felt completely transported into another reality, into a world where everything was possible and she was in control of everything that happened in her life. Sebastian weaved his magic spell over the audience, making new worlds of possibility appear out of thin air. Hanna felt like she was expanding. It was something truly new and wonderful, something she had never experienced before.

Sebastian finished his speech and invited the audience to raise questions. Hanna's mind was whirling with the imagery his words had created, and she was overcome with the intensely pleasurable feeling that the sound of his voice had created inside her. Some guy was rambling on about something, his ugly vowels a harsh contrast to Sebastian's, and Hanna blocked his sound out in order to savour the moment longer. Her entire body felt alive, vibrating, as if his voice had been plucking her strings, creating perfect harmonies.

Some minutes later, Hanna realised she had to get up and go, as the seminar room was almost empty. She was standing outside the room's double doors, smiling dreamily and thinking about what she had just heard and felt, when she heard someone calling her name.

'Hanna? Over here, I need to introduce you to someone!' Micheál's voice chirped from the bar. Through a small gap in between the masses of people, she was able to make out his slim, well-groomed form, wiggling in all directions. She weaved her way through the excited crowd to where Micheál was standing. There she was stopped in her tracks by the overpoweringly gorgeous smile of none other but *the* Sebastian O'Reilly himself. And he was looking at her. She found it difficult to breathe.

How did Micheál always manage to instantly become BFFs with the most interesting person in the room? He had an uncanny ability to be always in the right place at the right time.

Hanna had noticed at the start of the speech that Sebastian was handsome in a pretty-boy sort of fashion, but hadn't really paid much attention to his looks thereafter. She had been transfixed by his tantalising and mysterious words, and by the sound of his voice. The full power of Sebastian's physicality hit her only now. On stage, he had been cloaked in a charismatic energy bubble, which swirled around him, following his every elegant step. It hadn't dawned on her that he was a real person, someone that she could possibly ever talk to. He had merely been a conduit for amazing knowledge – godlike, completely unattainable.

But now he was standing here, right in front of her, and Hanna could feel something strange happening inside her. The room went quiet. He was real, flesh and blood, very much a man.

And he was looking at her with the most intense expression in his eyes. Sebastian's black, wavy hair was shiny; his Irish marble skin was translucent, his cheeks flushed and lips soft and red – all of which shouldn't look so good on a man. She was becoming rapidly even shorter of breath, and began to worry she would swoon – something she had never done before, not being the fainting-flower type. Luckily, Micheál grabbed her arm and pulled her to stand beside him, keeping her supported. She couldn't understand what was happening to her. As if from a faraway place, she heard Micheál speak:

'Sebastian, this is Hanna. She's from Finland, and she works as the *premier* piano tuner in the National Concert Hall,' Micheál introduced her in his typical over-the-top manner. She felt herself blush. She had been named, as if it were for the first time. Everything felt new; it was as if she was back to her first teenage dance, trying to talk to the boy she liked. What on earth was happening?

Micheál kept pulling at her ragdoll body, and Hanna soon found herself in front of him, directly under Sebastian's mesmerising blue-gray gaze. Hanna could do nothing but stare right into his eyes. There was no chance of her being able to pull her gaze away from his. She could hear that Micheál was still jabbering away to Sebastian, but the actual words escaped her notice. Beautiful colours were flashing through her mind. Nor did Sebastian seem to be interested in what Micheál was saying. He seemed to be leaning towards her, like a gently swaying birch tree in the insistent tug of a summer breeze.

She could suddenly feel all of her body. Heat was racing through her. She wanted him. Her first thought was to hide it, to turn around, to disappear. But that was not possible. The packed crowd kept pushing her closer to Sebastian, and Hanna found herself pressed against his chest. She had her right forearm up against his torso, and she felt as if she was on fire. Against her arm, she felt his heartbeat, and thrilled to feel his pulse elevated with her own.

'Hello,' said the celestial sound from above her. 'Nice to meet you, Hanna.'

Hanna couldn't speak. He felt divine. He smelled great, too: a nice, natural, masculine smell with just a hint of something additional. Sebastian seemed to have picked up on her mood, and felt no need to make conversation – a task that would have been nearly impossible anyhow, with the noise of the bar and all the people in it. Looking at him, she was transported back to the mystical world he had conjured on stage: the world of endless possibilities. Delicious possibilities.

He eventually asked for her phone number, which she gave him, her heart sounding like a percussionist on acid. She couldn't believe her luck. The place was so packed that twisting her body and her left arm to write the number onto a napkin at the bar required all her acrobatic skills. All the while, she was acutely aware of his body pressed against her left side. The task completed, and after some further glorious and unbelievable lounging against his chest, a sort of malformed Irish-style queue had built up around them of all the people who were dying to talk to Sebastian, with dagger looks being thrown in her direction at an ever-increasing pace. Sebastian reluctantly excused himself, removed her very unwilling body from his suction-like personal sphere and left Hanna standing there, with a final throwaway comment of, 'I'll call you'.

Hanna felt an almost physical pain when Sebastian removed himself. She stood there for a couple of minutes, abandoned, feeling the chill of separation from the heavenly creature, before Micheál suggested that they make tracks and go home. He guided Hanna puppeteer-like to the Luas stop, as she seemed to have lost her ability to give her body rational commands about where to go and what to do. She sat on the Luas, stunned, while Micheál happily chatted away about the evening, without seeming to notice that she hadn't said a word. But that was one of the best things about Micheál: one could be quiet in his company when no words were forthcoming.

## *Chapter 2*

Sebastian woke unusually early, on a high after his return to speak in front of a home audience in Dublin, and was in his office even before his assistant, the always-so-super-efficient Cathy. The office overlooked the River Liffey in Temple Bar, and the sun streamed in through the high sash windows of the old building. In the unexpected peace of the empty rooms, Sebastian relaxed and allowed himself to think back over the triumph of his performance.

He had really enjoyed himself last night. He always did, but before the event he had felt a special anticipation, as if something great was going to happen. His energy had buzzed around him, almost palpable. He had felt so clear, like a fully charged battery. The audience had been thinking hard, trying to decipher the meaning behind his words, some nodding their heads, some looking up at him in what appeared to be some sort of trance, their mouths hanging open in a perfect "O". The first few times this had happened, he hadn't quite known how he should react to it, so strange it had seemed. Now it felt normal.

He had noticed that particularly in the past two years or so, the audience seemed to be more and more on the same page as him, as theories of the structure of personal reality began to have an impact in the world. *The Secret* had been a magnificent moment for the latest wave of new-age theories, and he had been excited by its success. It had made his speeches and personal coaching services also more popular, allowing him to relax and indulge himself full time in the area of self-discovery. Sebastian always discovered more aspects of himself while working, keeping him permanently excited. He was truly blessed.

Sebastian felt complete. The words had flowed easily, and the audience felt positively charged. He felt energized. Boy, he loved his job!

'Sebastian, you're early. Well done last night.' Cathy's greeting, as she stopped outside the door of his office, broke into his reverie.

'Yeah, what a night!' said Sebastian. 'I'm still buzzing from it. There's nothing like talking to a large, live audience. And the questions they were asking were great – no nutjobs this time.'

'Yes, it was amazing. You were on fire up on that stage. I haven't seen you that enthusiastic for a while, even though you're always on form.'

'Thanks, Cathy, I felt great up there. And I want to do it again! There's something very special about being accepted in my own home town. I know a lot of people still regard what I do as crazy, and that's okay – but the support I got yesterday was amazing. You could really feel the positive buzz in the room.'

'You're just so gifted at this. The way you can put it into words is just – ah, so good.'

‘You’ve always been my biggest supporter. I don’t think I can ever sufficiently thank you for all you have done for me over the years.’

Cathy beamed at Sebastian, lapping up the compliments. ‘It’s a team effort. I need you – and you need me. Better get back to work now – I have a lot to do this morning with that event in Cork. It is great to be touring Ireland for a change. We’ve spent so much time in England recently.’

‘Yes, it is, isn’t it?’ Sebastian replied, leaning back on his seat, his hands joined on top of his head. His “power pose”, he had christened it. And he felt powerful today. *That girl last night...*

Cathy breezed past Sebastian, towards her own adjoining office. Her eyes were glued to Sebastian. He had pretty much made it clear that he adored her, and that was exactly how she wanted it. Everything was right on track: he was slowly coming around to understanding that he was hers, she was sure of it. Sebastian was just a true professional, and that’s why he hadn’t proposed anything to her yet – he was worried about how it would affect their working relationship. Cathy would just have to show him, slowly, that it was okay, and that they could have a professional and a personal relationship at the same time. Sometimes she felt anxious about how long it was taking Sebastian to realise this, but she was nothing if not a patient woman.

'Hello, folks! What a night!' Tim bumbled in through the door. Cathy sighed heavily. Tim was Sebastian's cameraman, but he was so clumsy, it was hard to believe that he was able to film anything at all. And yet he did it so well – if he had been any less perfect for the job, Cathy would have insisted a long time ago that Sebastian got rid of him. She couldn't understand why Sebastian tolerated Tim: he was like a happy little puppy, slobbering all over the place. *Such an idiot*, she thought.

'Morning, Tim,' said Sebastian. 'Yes, it was great – did you get it all? I'd like to see the footage as soon as possible – relive the night!' Sebastian enthused, doing a mini-jig with his feet under the table. He had been an Irish dancer growing up, and his feet often expressed his joy for him.

*All movement looks simply divine when Sebastian does it*, Cathy thought, irritated that Tim was not more like Sebastian. Tim's attempts to imitate Sebastian's moves only ever looked ridiculous.

'Yes, it's all safe and sound here,' Tim said, patting his camera bag, hopping happily from foot to foot. A jig it was not. Cathy rolled her eyes. She couldn't stand him, nor his stupid ever-present laugh, which could be heard anywhere at the most inopportune moment. And she couldn't stand his strong inner-city Dublin accent. The guy could at least try to make an effort to speak properly. Like Sebastian, whose accent was immaculate: just the way an Irish accent should sound, deliciously soft but always well-spoken.

'Excellent,' said Sebastian. 'Let me know when you have it ready and we'll watch it together. Cathy, isn't it great to have Tim on board? He's such a bundle of positive energy! I don't think I know anyone who is happier than Tim. Such a great example to us all.'

'Yes, it is good to have him,' Cathy said through gritted teeth. Tim, an example! Now she'd heard it all. 'Sebastian, I really need to get down to business now.'

'Yes, thanks, Cathy. What would we boys do without you?' Sebastian smiled at her. Cathy's heart melted. She did love him so.

'Yes, Cathy,' Tim lisped. 'What would we do without you?' Cathy could only shrug her shoulders, sigh and turn on her heel.

'She's a cold one, isn't she?' Tim said to Sebastian, his grin widening still further.

'She's a bit stressed sometimes, that's all. But it's that seriousness in her that makes her such a good PA. She's the only reason why the two of us have a job, let's not forget that.'

'No, let's not! And I *do* think she's so great! But I think she's never going to like me. What do you think?' For the first time, Tim's smile faltered.

'Of course she'll like you. As I keep saying, one of these days she's going to wake up and smell the coffee that is you. And we know how much she loves her coffee.' Sebastian smiled.

Tim's face flushed bright pink. Blasted Celtic skin! It always gave his thoughts away. 'Yes, coffee I am. I just adore her so much. She's the most amazing woman I've ever met, and I wish she'd hurry up and notice me.'

Tim had loved Cathy from afar for so long now. Although he had only worked for Sebastian for the best part of a year, the torment he felt over Cathy made it feel a lot longer. 'You know whe was the main reason I offered to start filming your seminars for you.'

'And there was me thinking that you thought what I had to say was so great!' Sebastian laughed.

'It is great, you know that! But I'm really just a trad musician, not a proper videographer. I remember going to your seminar in London just over a year ago, and when I saw Cathy introducing you, I knew I was gone. Just like that. It was weird.' Tim warmed up to his favourite topic. 'I never thought love could be like that – or at least unrequited love – but there it is. I knew I had to do something to keep in touch.' The grin was back. Tim just couldn't stay down for too long, lovesick or not.

‘Ah, my pride is wounded, but I can’t stay mad at you. In fact, I met a girl last night after the event and I think I might know what you mean by love at first sight.’

‘Oh, wow – the mighty Sebastian O’Reilly in love! Who is she?’

‘A girl from Finland, believe it or not. She works as a piano tuner in the concert hall. I got her phone number and I think I’ll give her a ring later on.’ *Definitely.*

‘You’re a stud, man. Way to go!’

‘Thanks. She had something special about her...’ Sebastian mused.

‘What are we like, mooning over the ladies? If only I could get Cathy to hear me play the guitar sometime, perhaps she’d change her mind about me.’

‘We’ll just have to organise it in such a way that she will hear you play, then! You are a man of many talents.’

‘Well, thanks for the compliment,’ said Tim. ‘Why don’t I invite you guys to one of my gigs? We’ll need to come up with some story to get Cathy along, though – I don’t think she would come if she knew it was to hear me play.’

‘Do you think so? She does behave oddly around you, I must admit. We’ll come up with something. Just let me know when you have a gig on and I'll work on getting her to it. Hey, maybe she secretly loves you already and that's why she's so strange with you,' Sebastian teased.

'I wish. I think she just doesn't like me, is all. But thanks, Sebastian – you're the best.' Delighted by the prospect of a chance to move things along with Cathy, Tim felt more hopeful than he had done in a long time.

*

'Bing, bing, bing...' Mechanically adjusting the tuning lever as she continuously hit the note, Hanna was listening with only half an ear. Her mind was elsewhere, busily dissecting the events of the previous night. Today was the most important day of the whole year, the one day at work when she really needed to be sharp. She had eight concert grand pianos on the stage to tune together – no mean feat. Hanna had been anticipating this event for months, in equal measures of excitement and terror.

It was the most exciting concert of the season, a spectacular show of talent, featuring all of the previous winners of the Dublin Piano Competition. To even source eight full-size concert grand pianos had been difficult in a country as small as Ireland, let alone organising the concert that would feature so many on stage at once. The regular Dublin Concert Hall tuner, David, had been mightily upset when he had heard that he was going to be missing all the fun. He had never done it before either, and doubted that he'd ever get the opportunity again. Hanna wished fervently that she was back in her own safe little piano world in Helsinki, where David was now doing her job, rather than here in the middle of this nightmare scenario.

It was a tough job for a piano technician to match even two pianos together. The concert organisers hadn't been even remotely sensible in giving her only two days to get them all tuned. But Hanna had become accustomed to the fact that nobody really understood anything about her work. She usually liked to take her time with her pianos; she was very proud of her skill, and hated letting go of an instrument before it was perfect. She could easily have spent at least a full day on each piano, but she had quickly realised it would be futile to even try to suggest anything like it. Two days was more than she had expected. But today was the one day of her entire working career when she couldn't concentrate at all. It wasn't fair.

Hanna made a massive effort to focus again and got through the middle section of the piano. *Next, the base, then the unisons and then the treble. Only 88 keys which consist of 220 strings to tune... per piano. Not to mention voicing the hammers and regulating the actions. Oh boy*. She was never going to make it. Hanna's stomach was responding to her high emotions, her mind racing with ideas. And none of those ideas had anything to do with pianos or tuning.

Sebastian.

And his magical speech.

And his glorious being.

He had opened up entirely new worlds for her. Her mind was busy assimilating all his new ideas, processing his words on the meaning of emotions. Her body, quite separately, was working on an intense programme of remembering of its own. Sebastian had explained that emotions were simply energy in motion, nothing more, nothing less. *How did it go again*? thought Hanna, her mind far away from her work.

She was so confused. She'd be more than happy to be kept back in class to hear Sebastian explain it all over again... he could explain it all to her for the rest of her life, as far as she was concerned. Hanna blushed, highly entertained by her wonderful thoughts of *him*. He was dreamy. Would he call?

'Hello, Hanna. How are the pianos coming on?'

'Oh, hi Barry!' said Hanna. *Where had he come from?* 'Ummm, they are coming along just fine,' she fibbed quickly, her heart in her throat from the scare the floor manager's unexpected presence had given her. 'I should be finishing up the tuning on this one in the next couple of minutes – and then I just need to tone a couple of notes. Then I'll move onto the next.' *Gosh, this was all just too hard today*!

'That's grand! Keep up the good work, so!' said Barry O'Hara, coming up to the piano. He leaned on it in a manner that irritated Hanna massively, stamping it with his paw marks – all of which Hanna would have to clean up later. In an ideal world, nobody would ever get to touch her beautiful pianos – not even to play them.

'Did you go to that talk yesterday in the end, by that fellah, Sebastian-something?' Barry was still booming, even though he was now standing beside Hanna. Irish people were so irritatingly loud at times. And they always stood too close to her. And they moved too much, most foreigners did, in fact. Hanna was still shocked by it all, a lot of the time, although she should have been used to it by now. She could hear the piano humming to the sound of Barry's loud voice.

Her heart was also humming, but to quite a different tune. *Sebastian*. Something a bit more erratic was happening inside her. She felt the colour creeping up her neck and her cheeks again: hearing Sebastian's name mentioned out loud had been quite shocking. The name had been singing in her brain all night and morning, but it was somehow wrong to hear it spoken out loud by someone else. She felt almost naked. She tried to keep her voice light and casual as she said, 'Sebastian O'Reilly? Yes, it was great – I really enjoyed myself. He was a very good speaker, and Micheál and I stayed quite late afterwards at the bar. I think I will go again.'

'Well, well, missy – are you blushing? I haven't seen you colour up like that before – and you look suspiciously cheery. No serious frown on your face today! Did you meet someone? Wait, I know: it's the man himself, isn't it – he's a good looking guy now. You're not falling for a bit of positive mumbo jumbo now, are you? Well?'

Hanna coloured up even further, quite involuntarily, trying very hard to maintain her cool exterior. It was not working: nothing was functioning properly today.

'Ah, this is class. Our prim and proper Miss Finland falling for a chancer-charmer Paddy! Wait 'til they hear this upstairs!' The potentially juicy bit of scandal got him moving again, and he was pounding off the stage before Hanna could stop him.

'Wait!' Hanna called after him, but to no avail. Barry was off with the gossip. Whether it was true or not didn't really seem to be the point – although in this case he had actually hit the nail on the head. Hanna had fallen last night – almost literally keeled over, into Sebastian's arms, purely with the shock of being in his presence. She had become a believer.

Now, there was a first: she had been attracted to men before – had had boyfriends, flings, the whole shebang – but she had never expected to be quite literally knocked off her feet. *How am I going to stop Barry before he tells the whole crew of the NCH that I have fallen for "a guy off the telly"? Mission impossible*, she answered herself, and began to prepare herself to bear the consequences.

*

It turned out to be a gruelling day at work. Naturally, Barry did his worst, and Hanna did not hear the end of it all day. The piano work had not been any better, and she still had a tonne left to do. It hadn't helped that everyone from the staff of the concert hall had managed to come up with some excuse or another to drop in on her, most of them pretending at first to be interested in the spectacular sight of so many grand pianos on the stage at the same time.

There had been a lot of snide remarks about an Irishman never being good enough for someone from the "perfect" country of Finland, all the while pretending that they were not talking about Hanna per se but discussing the topic in general. Hanna's enthusiastic (and, she now admitted to herself, perhaps a tad self-righteous) explanations about Finland and how things worked there – as opposed to nothing working in Ireland – had obviously been interpreted in a different light than that which she had intended. She had only been stating facts, when describing the way buses were always on time in Finland, and how there was no litter or no crime, and how everyone adhered to the law. It had obviously not gone down very well with her fellow workers. Not that the polite

Irish would ever let on that they didn't appreciate her manner of explanation – until today. Payback *was* a bitch.

Only one time before had the staff at the NCH made fun of her enthusiastic explanations, finding the fact that her mother had kept her up to date with the latest new laws – so that she could continue being a perfect citizen upon her return – hilarious. Hanna had thought this was a perfectly sensible thing to do, and a worthy topic of conversation.

Her well-intended-but-massively-misinterpreted frankness about the superiority of all things Finnish had backfired. She had been too tired of it all to point out that the "payback to the Vikings" her colleagues were chuckling over was, strictly speaking, inaccurate given that the Finns had never been Vikings – only worked for them. It would have been pointless, and they would simply have twisted all her well-meaning explanations into something else again. She'd learned some hard lessons on cultural differences today, on top of everything. *On the bright side, I must be truly accepted as part of the team now*, she thought grimly, as it was the first time she had been so cruelly abused at work since arriving in Ireland just over a year ago.

She had by chance found the Irish piano tuner, David O'Brien, whose contract the Dublin Concert Hall gig actually was, on the Internet a year and a half ago. They had got on famously, discussing piano work in great detail, and as they had realised that they both had the same job in their respective countries – Hanna usually worked at the Helsinki Concert Hall – they had come up with the idea of doing the two-year work exchange they were currently in the middle of.

It had taken a bit of organising to get their respective organisations on board with the idea, but they had persisted and had managed to pull it off in the end. They kept in touch via email and Skype, and enjoyed comparing their individual culture shocks. Her colleague David could not get over the daytime matter-of-factness of the Finns, contrasting with their complete willingness to get more sloshed than should be possible during their nights out and losing all vestiges of decorum completely – some extremists, he had called them. No wonder the Finns were good at all the mad sports, such as Formula 1, ice hockey and ski jumping. 'And have you ever heard of ice-swimming: now, what is *that* all about?' David exclaimed one night in horrible fascination.

Hanna learned a lot about her own culture from her Skype chats with David. She also had to consult with him on more than one occasion about some Irish expressions she kept hearing – such as "it's just a bit of *craíc*", or why everything was always so "grand". Her English was rapidly becoming littered with Irish expressions, and she was enjoying the relaxed atmosphere. Perhaps it was not so great when you wanted to get something done, but so refreshing on so many new levels: it was a great relief for Hanna to learn that life didn't have to be taken so seriously all the time.

Time enough for that when she went back to Finland in a few months.

Hanna's phone rang and she nearly dropped her tuning lever, which she had been just about to put on yet another tuning pin. Her heart was racing from the shock of the noise as well as from the fact that she had nearly damaged the piano. She was a nervous wreck today. She picked up the phone with shaking hands and answered the call.

'Hanna? This is Sebastian O'Reilly. How are you?'

'Um, I'm fine.' *Oh my God*, thought Hanna. *He phoned me! The one and only, dreamy Sebastian O'Reilly actually called me! Quickly, think of something intelligent to say... ah, nothing coming to mind.*

'Um, how are you?'

*How original, but buys me time... what else could I possibly say? Oh God, he's saying something now*!

'...nice to meet you the other night. Your friend Micheál certainly is a pushy fellah, but I can't be too upset as it meant that I got to meet you. Would you like to go out for a drink sometime?' Sebastian's voice was gloriously resonant even over the phone.

'Um, I'd love to.'

*I have to stop humming and hawing now! Pull yourself together, woman*, Hanna told herself. *You are a modern, independent woman: you can't get flustered every time this man speaks to you. This is not Victorian England.*

*Oh, but what a man*. Hanna could feel the blush creeping up on her cheeks again. He had the strangest effect on her, both mentally and physically; she had never had to deal with anything like this before. Her dreams had been full of him, as well as her waking moments. She had been in some sort of a daze, her imagination efficient in supplying endless beautiful situations: him whispering wonderful words into her ear in that gorgeous voice, his eyes upon her, assessing her admiringly... *hold on, what is that sound? Yikes, he's still there, on the phone, talking*!

'Hanna? Are you there? I was just saying that I'd love to meet up with you this Saturday, if that was to suit you? Where do you live? I could pick you up and bring you to this little pub I know up in the Dublin mountains where we can have a good chat. Would you like that?'

'That would be fine. Um, I live in Rathfarnham – where do you live?' Hanna managed to say, pleased with how normal her voice sounded. She didn't feel normal; in fact, she felt that she had been disembodied and haphazardly reassembled, and she did not yet entirely understand how her parts fitted together.

'I live in Rathgar, so that's perfect. Rathfarnham is on the way. Can you text me your exact address and I'll see you then, let's say, around 8 p.m.?'

'Yes, that's fine. See you on Saturday, then.' Hanna finished with a brisk business-like manner, trying to hide her fluttering heart. Sebastian said goodbye again in that endless Irish staccato of "byes" and at last, he was gone. Hanna could let the panic take over!

*Ohmygod, ohmygod, ohmygod*!

*He phoned me! Sebastian O'Reilly asked me out!*

*On a date! I can't believe it*!

*But what will I wear?* The panic was setting in again.

## *Chapter 3*

*Saturday.*

*Sebastian Day.*

Hanna woke up with a start. Sebastian was going to come and take her out on a date tonight! She felt like a princess waiting for her Prince Charming. It didn't feel real.

"Butterflies" wasn't an apt enough description for the tension she was feeling in her gut. It was more like eggs jumping around in boiling water, crashing into each other. She could feel herself shaking. Hanna could not remember ever having such a strong physical reaction to a man before, and this realisation was battering her fragile composure even further.

At last she was able to relate to her counterparts in Georgette Heyer's world: all those fluttering women who had seemed so silly to her, although very entertaining, when she had gone through an intense Heyer reading period. Now she was one of them. She half-expected a maid to bring in the hot chocolate and fling open the curtains any minute, with a cheerful 'Good morning, Miss Hanna!'

No hot chocolate having magically appeared, she hauled herself out of bed and waddled into the bathroom. A concert was in full voice outside her bathroom window, as the summer birds chirpily flitted from tree to tree. The high-pitched sounds reminded her of the previous night's concert, and she sighed heavily. It had been terrible. But incredibly, nobody had seemed to notice anything. The pianos had been awful – not exactly screaming out of tune, but not far off. She had never felt so embarrassed in her life. Every note was like needles pricking her skin and she was exhausted by the end of it.

It was a curse to have such an acute understanding of the correct piano sound – it made enjoying piano music so much more difficult. She could only ever fully appreciate concerts for which she had ample time to tune and service the instrument fully. Despite the many talented pianists at last night's concert, all she had been able to hear was the wrongness in the sound, inevitably leading her to agonise over what she would do to improve it. It had been horrific.

Anyway: she had got through it, and it was over.

The view of the garden and its numerous trees was magnificent, and she found great solace in this. Irish gardens were normally so bare. She felt so lucky that her colleague David, who owned the house, shared her personal views regarding trees: the more the better.

Hanna felt the anticipation of the night ahead rise again inside her. *Sebastian.* And the weather had also favoured Sebastian Day. Although what else could be expected, when it came to him:

he seemed to live a charmed life, his wonderful imaginings creating an aura of joyful mystery.

What was it about him that Hanna felt so drawn to? He was good-looking, yes, but it was more than that. Something within her seemed to resonate with his entire being, not just his words and smiles. Was she flattered about his supposed celebrity status? It was nice, but since she had never even heard of him before Tuesday's event, it couldn't be just that. At some level, there was a connection between them that she couldn't explain, a connection that was evident even from their brief encounter. Let's face it: she had hardly even exchanged a word with him. His speech the other night had affected her deeply – there was no denying that – but his true impact had been in her introduction to him, in their body language. And something more… Drifting back to reality from her constant daydreaming, Hanna realised with a shock that she only had a few hours to get her clothes and face together for her date. Time to hit the shops.

*

Countless discarded looks later, Hanna returned home, tired but pleased, an outfit bought and paid for. Conscious of drawing increasingly stranger glances from the sales assistants, easily-embarrassed Hanna had changed shops a few times after one too many frantic dives into the depths of the changing rooms with her arms full of clothes. She had eventually settled for red and black, in a chic-but-sexy-look – revealing little, promising more. At least, she hoped that's how it would be interpreted.

She showered and blow-dried her brown hair, enhanced with the aid of as many chemicals as she had been able to persuade it to accept. She had been surprised to find out when she moved to Ireland that her boring, dead straight, incredibly fine hair was highly coveted. At home, mad curls had been a must when she was a teenager, and many Finns still thought so nowadays. Having been brought up believing curly was great, she often sighed with jealousy when a particularly beautiful head of curls – often in the coveted red colour – presented itself to her. But it was Sebastian's typically Irish taste – she hoped – that she wanted to appeal to tonight.

She was putting the final touches to her makeup when she heard the doorbell. *He can't be here yet*! Hanna thought in panic. It was only half past seven, and he had definitely said eight o'clock. She tried to peep through the curtains inconspicuously, and to her relief saw Micheál dancing around at her front door. The boy never stayed still if he could help it.

'Micheál, what are you doing? You shouldn't be here, you know that! Sebastian is going to be here in a minute and I have to get ready!' Hanna squeaked through the upstairs window.

'Oh, hello to you also, sweetheart. Let me in – you need someone to check you out before your very special date. You know

I have impeccable taste, and you need my opinion. Hurry up and open this door! Oh, never mind – I'll just use my own key.'

Hanna rushed down the stairs to stop Micheál from barging in, but she was too late. He was already standing in the hall, with a huge grin on his face.

'You look wonderful, darling. I didn't think you had it in you – the fashion sense, I mean. You never really dress up. Well done!' Micheál enthused, his appraising eye sweeping her from top to toe.

'Thanks. I'm a total bag of nerves. I don't know why. I'm not looking for a boyfriend. I mean, I'm going back to Finland soon, my future is there, so I can't see how a long distance relationship could work. No sane Irish person could possibly want to move to Finland, and – no offence – I can't see myself staying here long term. Although the place is growing on me.'

'Relax, Hanna! You're not getting married; it's just a date with a hunk. You're supposed to enjoy it.' Micheál flustered around, fixing Hanna's hair, pulling invisible lint off her outfit and generally harassing her, until she gave him such a look that he stopped.

Hanna sighed heavily. 'I just haven't been on a date in such a long time, and never with someone who has had this kind of effect on me. Are you sure I look OK? Or should I put my hair up?' Hanna was dangerously close to panic.

'Whoa, slow down! You look great; didn't I just tell you that? So this guy really means a lot to you, does he now? I told you he was perfect for you.' Micheál began working himself up into pat-my-own-back mode.

'Yes, Micheál, you did say that, but now – get over it. You have to help me. What do I say to him, what are the dos and don'ts? I've never dated an Irishman before. Give me some tips, you should know.'

'Okay, okay, I'll help you. And you're supposed to say "please" – haven't we talked about this before? The main thing to do is to smile. You have a tendency to frown a lot and not look very friendly. Must be your northern thing, but it doesn't necessarily come across very well here in Ireland, if I may say so. I was able to see through you, but I might have been thrown a bit with you in the early days, when you were just so horribly serious and tough all the time. I could have so easily believed that you didn't absolutely love me. So: smile! Show me now – time to practise. Chop, chop!'

Hanna gave him the best smile she was able to muster.

'Hmm, not great. Can't you do a bit better than that? I know he is Mr Positive, but he could also be a bit nervous on this date. He'll run a mile in a fright if you bare your teeth at him like that.'

'Argh, I'm just so nervous! How can I smile when I feel like I need to throw up? Talking of which – I think I need to use the loo again,' Hanna stated and promptly ran up the stairs.

*Young love. This is not going great. I hope she can relax a bit more, or she'll blow her chances with the Amazing Sebastian. And I really was starting to hope for great things from this guy*, Micheál thought to himself as he walked into the kitchen to get Hanna some water. *Sebastian could just be the missing link of my master plan to keep Hanna in Ireland for the long term*. Hanna needed more reasons to stay. She was always so annoyingly adamant in her belief that she was moving back to Finland soon. A nasty thought.

There was a knock on the door. Sebastian was early.

He must have Googled "Scandinavia", thought Micheál, and learned that the Nordics were always early. After a while, he went to open the door as there was no sign of Hanna.

'Hello, Sebastian! Great to see you again.' Micheál welcomed Sebastian in.

'Thanks. Um, is Hanna here?'

*Oh my God*, Micheál thought, *the boy is terrified. How can that be? At least that makes two of them...*

Sebastian looked very nervous, possessing none of the godlike composure and dazzling stage aura he had sported on the night of his talk. *He must really like our Hanna*, thought Micheál. *Excellent.*

'Yes, yes, she's just getting ready and will be down in a sec! *Suí síos*, and all that. Would you like a drink? I don't think Hanna has much choice in her fridge, but I can get you a glass of water, if you like? In fact, I have a fresh glass right here!' He offered him the glass he had just poured for Hanna.

'Thanks, that's great. Can I ask your name again? I know we met the night you introduced Hanna to me, but your name escapes me, I'm afraid.'

'Micheál, that's me. I'm Hanna's best friend, or at least I am since she moved to Ireland. I saw you recently on the telly, and thought that you would be a great guy for our Hanna to meet. That's why I dragged her down to your speech,' said Micheál.

'I got a really good feeling about Hanna straight away,' said Sebastian. 'She has this atmosphere of being brilliantly gifted, without being too aware of it.'

'Well, that's an excellent summary of our Hanna: aren't you quick? She's a fantastic pianist. You must get her to play to you.' Micheál enjoyed talking about one of his favourite topics. He adored Hanna.

'It's sort of a talent of mine, to be able to read people,' admitted Sebastian. 'I don't know what it is about her – and I don't even really know her yet – but I'm very drawn. "This girl, I gotta get to know", my brain seems to be saying to me.' He was smiling.

At that moment, they both heard Hanna coming down the stairs.

'Sorry about that, Micheál, I'm just so nervous. He's so gorgeous and I'm sort of frumpy. Do you really think I look oka...' Hanna's speech was cut short as she entered the kitchen and saw Sebastian. She felt herself colouring up desperately with embarrassment. He had arrived and she hadn't heard it. Good thing that Micheál had been there to open the door for him, otherwise he could have just left, and she wouldn't have got her date. Horrifying thought!

Sebastian got up and took Hanna by the hand, frozen in mid-air where she had come to a full stop at the door.

'Hi, Hanna. I'm nervous too. Good to hear that it makes two of us. I can relax now. And I hope it is good-nervous you're feeling – I'm really looking forward to tonight,' Sebastian smiled. 'You look fabulous!'

'Um, thanks – and it is good-nervous, I think. I didn't hear you come in.' Hanna was blushing, her face flooded with all her favourite shades of red.

Micheál jumped up. 'I'm off, so: have a really good night, you two, and I'll be wanting to hear everything tomorrow, Hanna.

Call me!' With this, Micheál ran out the door, banging it shut behind him. Hanna glared at his disappearing back.

'Wow, your friend Micheál is something else.' Sebastian was laughing now.

Hanna had to join in, though her laugh, she thought, was more like a nervous giggle. Horrendous. She blushed even deeper, if that was possible.

'Shall we go, then? I think you'll enjoy this little pub I go to from time to time – when I want to have a bit of quiet but fun time alone. It's not too far from here, about a 20-minute drive,' Sebastian said as he propelled Hanna towards the door. She seemed to have lost the power of speech and mobility. Again. Many a time during her trip to Ireland, she had felt that living in a foreign country turned one into a child again, everything new and hard to understand. She thought she had got quite used to this "child-adult" state, but these Sebastian-induced conscious blackouts were something else.

'Oh – I just have to lock the back door and grab my handbag!' Hanna remembered, and rushed back into the kitchen. The bolts in the back door had always been difficult to close and this evening they seemed particularly monstrous. The bottom one needed a good kick, and her new red heels didn't quite have the power required. Sebastian watched her for a while, then walked back into the kitchen and closed the bolts in a second. *Typical. This guy is brilliant at everything*, Hanna thought, feeling still more inadequate, and super-clumsy.

A few minutes later, they had left suburbia behind, and the car started to climb a small mountain road. Terrified, Hanna closed her eyes at every bend as Sebastian drove through the snake-roads of the Dublin mountains at top speed. *He does look very relaxed behind the wheel*, she thought to herself, trying to calm her nerves. Sebastian kept up a gentle flow of comments and questions, to which Hanna gave monosyllabic answers.

The trees on both sides of the road created a tunnel, making it almost pitch-dark. At times, branches touched the top of Sebastian's car with eerie scratching sounds. Hanna felt jumpy, and the ever-increasing bendiness of the ever-narrowing road did nothing to soothe her nerves. It was like a funfair ghost ride times ten.

'Are you all right?' Sebastian asked, turning to look at Hanna, who was sinking deeper into her seat by the minute, her eyes practically closed.

'Keep your eyes on the road! *Please*!' Hanna managed to remember her hard-learned English manners through her panic. No such thing as "please" in Hanna's native language. The word was most easily learned in Ireland, where it was so liberally applied to any situation that needed even a smudge of politeness. Even so, it had taken a long time for Hanna's brain to understand the meaning of a word that didn't exist in translation, and often, she simply forgot to use it.

'Are you nervous about the road? Is that why you're constantly closing your eyes?' Sebastian was smiling widely now, holding back laughter.

'Yes, I'm a bit nervous. You are going awfully fast, aren't you? What if a car comes – are you not going to crash?' Hanna asked in a small voice.

'Sorry – I'll slow down, if my speed makes you so uncomfortable. I know these roads so well that I didn't think I was going fast at all. I'm in such a good mood, so perhaps I am driving a bit faster than is necessary. I *so* want to show you this place.'

'Thanks. I've just never seen a road like this before in my life. Finnish roads are always very wide. This road would be a total impossibility over there – in the wintertime, it would be impassable.' Hanna found her voice at last.

'It does get icy here in the winter too, as we are so high up. But tell me more about Finland – I've never been there. What is it like?' Sebastian was gently probing her to continue talking, since she had finally managed a full sentence.

'Finland? Well, my Irish colleague, David, has told me lots of interesting things about the country that I've never really thought about. Over 70% of it is forest, and over 10% lakes. Most of the country is untouched nature.'

'Wow, sounds amazing! So many trees – I love trees.'

'The forests and the general look of the landscape are so different from Ireland. Irish trees are much bigger, like here now on this road. And we mostly have conifers, pine and spruce – Christmas trees.' Hanna scrunched up her face, thinking hard, all of Micheál's well-intended advice about smiling forgotten.

'I can see some oaks here now,' continued Hanna, 'but what do you call that beautiful tree with the light green leaves and the silver bark?'

'I think it's a beech. I love the way they create those amazing tunnels of green over the road. I think I like to come to this pub so much not just for the place itself, but also because of this spectacular drive.'

'It is pretty special. Particularly now I can actually see the trees and not just a green blur flying past me.' Hanna had calmed down enough to be able to tease Sebastian a little.

'I have to say, you have an amazing command of the English language.'

'Thanks. It normally drives me crazy when people compliment my English,' admitted Hanna, 'but somehow it doesn't sound so bad coming from your mouth. I always seem to take it the wrong way – secretly, I always believe they actually think my English is quite poor. And it makes me feel separate, labelled as different, when all I'm trying to do is fit in.' Hanna sighed. 'I'm a "listener" by profession,' she continued, 'as you know. Foreign languages have always interested me, especially English. I love to listen to the way they sound. I've always had English-speaking friends, in particular in the musical circles in Helsinki, so I was never *not* speaking English, if you know what I mean!' Hanna was able to laugh now briefly.

'Well, we should suit each other very well, then, as I'm a "talker" by profession,' grinned Sebastian.

He managed to tease a smile out of Hanna. She looked beautiful, he thought, when she wasn't being so serious.

Being with Sebastian was starting to feel very good for Hanna. She had finally got over her nerves. She could feel a wonderful bubbling starting in her tummy. Definitely not nerves, but something a lot more delicious.

*

'Here we are: *fáilte*!' Sebastian guided Hanna into a quiet, private corner booth at the back of the little pub. 'What would you like to drink?'

'I don't actually drink alcohol any more. I gave up after my last birthday.' Hanna wasn't going to confess that this had only been a few days ago. 'Can I have lemonade or something?'

'I don't actually drink either – I just come here for the atmosphere. Excuse me a minute,' Sebastian said and dashed off in the direction of the bar. *A non-drinker*, he thought. What a rare find! But weren't the Finns supposed to be very heavy drinkers? Mind you, the Irish also had that reputation, but he had never taken to it. He had tried to drink alcohol in his teens, like everyone else, but had quite literally spat it out and vowed never to go there again.

While Hanna waited for Sebastian to come back, she looked around the small but charming pub. The theme was obviously "Olde Worlde barn", or something like it; there was sawdust on the ground, and the walls were hung with all sorts of weird and wonderful stuff. Hanna could see night pans, old timber rakes, and other strange paraphernalia. The cheerful *diddly-o* tunes of Irish music were coming from the other room, where the bar was, and she found her foot tapping along to the rapid, cheerful beat of the music.

She had fallen in love with Irish music when she first heard it in her teens, and had wanted to visit Ireland ever since. She had managed to get her hands on some Irish piano music, composed and arranged by Phil Coulter, and had spent many hours tinkling away at such classics as the *Spinning Wheel* and *Danny Boy*. She felt that a place where the music was so happy must be a place for people who were also very happy. She had loved the idea of the two-year job-swap, and had literally danced her version of an Irish reel the day she found out that they could actually make it happen. And her assumptions had been right: the Irish were a cheery bunch. They had made Hanna feel so very welcome. *And talking about cheerful Irishmen: look at the smile on that one coming towards me now.*

'Cheers, big ears!' Sebastian said as they clinked their glasses together.

'What did you say? I've never heard that one before!' Hanna couldn't hold her laugh back. Her nerves had disappeared, replaced with simple, relaxed contentment, spiced with a frisson of excitement through her lower stomach every now and again. Sebastian oozed such easy-going relaxation that it was hard to hold onto any tension, and Hanna was thoroughly enjoying herself.

He had a charming way of moving his head from side to side to mark his most emphatic comments that made her fall in love with him even more. She knew she was doomed with this perfect man – it could never work – but she couldn't care less. Time for awfulness later (hopefully much later). For once, she decided to just go with the flow, rather than plan her entire life in order to know how to get through the next five minutes. Sebastian was here now, clearly trying very hard to entertain her, and she was grateful.

'Cheers, big ears? You never heard that? It's a classic. Or, maybe it's just something we used to say when we were kids, with my sisters. I can't actually remember who started to say it first, but it kind of stuck with us. I have two younger sisters, not much younger than me, and we were a close-knit group – even though they were girls and I wasn't – up to our teens, when it all changed. We are close again now as adults, but we never got back to being really good friends, the way we were the first ten years or so,' Sebastian said, with a look of regret.

'That's sad,' said Hanna sympathetically. 'I have a sister, but she's five years younger than me. We were never that close because of the age gap, even though we played a lot together. She's quite different from me, and she still lives back in my hometown of Turku.'

'Where is that?'

'About 160 kilometres west of Helsinki – that's where I studied, and now work. Or *worked*, rather – before I came to Ireland. I'm due to go back to Finland in about six months, and I intend to enjoy it as much as possible before I return to the cold,' said Hanna, shivering involuntarily at the thought.

*So, I have six months with her to work my magic: good to know*. 'Is it really cold there all the time? I've never been to

Finland. To be honest, I don't really know much at all about the country, apart from some Googling this week.'

'Nobody in Ireland knows anything about Finland. I'm well used to it by now. No, it's only cold during the winter, which does seem to go on forever – but summers can be absolutely fabulous. I gather that Irish summers aren't usually as great as the one we've been having?'

'No, this has been exceptional. Tell me more about the Finnish summer.' Sebastian loved the sound of Hanna's accent – matter of fact, with the words very precisely pronounced without much inflection within the low pitch. She seemed to highlight her vowels, which sounded exotic to his ears. And the way she pronounced "Finland" was funny: she stressed the start of the word a lot, but pronounced the second syllable quite separately, with the "a" a strong "au" sound.

'The light levels are great! Brightness until midnight in the south, and 24 hours of sunshine in Lapland.'

Sebastian thought she looked especially beautiful at this moment, talking about her home country. *It must be tough for her to move abroad, having to fit in with the local language and customs*, he thought. He knew a bit about it from having lived in England for so long. He felt suddenly very protective towards her. Actually, he was feeling a whole bundle of things towards her, and all of them good. He was aware of an increasing urge to kiss her.

Would she think him too forward? He had heard that they were pretty liberal in Scandinavia, but did that apply to Hanna?

Hanna turned towards him with a dazzling smile on her lips, her eyes moist with the sudden happiness of being with Sebastian. She thought of the Finnish summer, brief but intense, its hectic energy deeply affecting the natives. It was pure enchantment – like Sebastian. Instinctively, she moved closer to him, even though they were already squashed together in what looked like a miniature church pew. She tilted her face up to look at him directly, a sunflower turning to the sun.

And then he kissed her.

It was heavenly.

His lips were soft and gentle. The tremor under the surface of her skin since she had first met Sebastian grew inside her, rapidly taking over her entire body. She felt his presence deep inside her, even though they were only kissing. Time had stopped. Hanna had lost all sense of space, apart from the Sebastian-space surrounding her, inside and around her.

At last, they drew apart. Hanna locked her gaze with his, and saw that his eyes were now almost black with desire. They were rimmed with dreamily long black lashes, the likes of which Hanna had only seen in foreign films. Sebastian's startlingly contrasting colours, marble skin and black hair, dark eyes and eyebrows with rosy cheeks and lips, created havoc in Hanna's core. *My Snow-White man*, she thought. Sebastian's look was so different from the faces she had grown up with. She was mesmerised, borne away on waves of attraction.

Sebastian gazed intently back into Hanna's green eyes, enjoying what he was seeing. Hanna's lightly tanned, smooth, freckle-free skin, and straight, brown hair were equally new and interesting to him. He found himself overwhelmed with an urge to stroke her fine hair, falling soft and smooth either side of her cute little face; her full lips looked plump and red, in their post-kiss state – and utterly re-kissable.

He was falling fast, and he was delighted. Sebastian had always been picky. He had become convinced that he'd never meet anyone like Hanna – someone who utterly enchanted him, someone who could affect him so deeply. He had been so careful with women, but with Hanna he felt a delightful recklessness taking over, and he was willing to do anything it took to get her. He was awed by the strength and intensity of his feelings, dormant for so long.

He resolved to go slowly; after all, she had just told him that he had six months to woo her. He didn't want to frighten Hanna, or do anything that might jeopardise their budding relationship. There was a possibility of something great here. Despite knowing so little about her, he was totally convinced that this was it: she was the one. It was as if he had found the last missing piece of the jigsaw that was him, and he was unwilling to lose it again.

*

Sebastian slept surprisingly well after his date with Hanna, considering the highly excited state he had been in when he had got home. It had taken a lot of willpower to find his calm again, through his mantras and highly focused breathing methods, but the years of practice had paid off, and he had enjoyed some satisfying dreams of highly exciting kissing, and more...

He woke around 11 a.m. and enjoyed a leisurely breakfast, accompanied by a podcast from one his favourite personal development speakers. His business of personal development coaching had emerged quite accidentally out of his passion for following his heart to change his own life, but it had grown steadily over the past number of years. Nowadays, he was often asked to be a speaker at all kinds of events, and had regular TV and radio work. He had even recently been asked to be the host of his own TV show – the icing on the cake. The idea behind the programme was to demonstrate to a wider audience his methods of working with people to transform their beliefs. Business was booming. He loved every minute of his working life, and now Hanna had appeared out of nowhere to sweeten things still further.

*Hanna... hmm... now, there was a real woman.* Sebastian found his thoughts brought quickly back to the hot topic. Even his favourite speaker, who normally had his whole attention, failed to break through this new glow of contentment and awareness of all things Hanna.

Sebastian wondered when would be a good time to phone her. The last thing he wanted to do was to freak her out by coming onto her too strong. He had so wanted to follow Hanna into her little house last night; it had taken every ounce of his self-control to turn around and walk back to his car. He wanted Hanna to know that he was a gentleman. So, he would pursue her gently... He still couldn't get over the fact that he barely knew anything about the girl who had entirely captured his attention. But his years of disciplined self-study had taught him to trust his gut feeling. Slow was good.

Now he just had to make sure that the feeling was mutual. Sebastian had never been in a serious relationship before, having shied away from it for many reasons – mostly because he wanted to maintain his independence, his freedom to come and go as he pleased, the freedom to explore his life. His freedom had always been the most important thing to him, but now he was not so sure. He wanted to take his time, to make sure he was making the right decision. Hanna had seemed pretty smitten with him; he remembered her look of utter amazement when he had wished her goodnight and gone home.

Sebastian would court her long and thoroughly, he decided. Hanna was so different from anyone else he had ever met; it was hard to read her signals. And he felt so much more for her than he had ever done before that it was frightening. He'd take his time. He wanted to be sure that his feelings were returned before fully committing to anything. He could feel the fear of getting too involved, just to have his heart ripped out.

## *Chapter 4*

'Sofia? You are not going to believe what has happened to me! I've met the man of my dreams! Actually he's more than that, he's perfect, so amazing...'

'Hanna? Calm down. I'm a bit busy now – I have three horses to wash and feed. I can pop over in about an hour? Can you wait that long?' Sofia was laughing on the phone.

'An hour? But I need to tell you about him *now* or I'll burst! He's the most amazing thing there is, he's just...'

'OK, OK, I got that. I'll be there as soon as possible, but it could be almost an hour. See you then.' Sofia hung up.

Hanna was left standing in her living room, frustratedly staring at her phone. She was like a cat on a hot tin roof, and couldn't sit still for a second. It was Sunday morning, the day after *the* date, and she hadn't really slept a wink last night.

She was high as a kite, head over heels in love. It was very scary.

Sebastian had dropped her off at her house just after one o'clock in the morning, after they had spent some more quality time kissing in the pub. And again in the car, up in a scenic stopover place in the mountains where they were supposed to have been watching the sparkly lights of Dublin city. They had glanced at them quickly and then got down to the more pressing business at hand. He had kissed her again outside her front door, to which he had walked her, as if they were in a mushy American movie. And then to Hanna's complete surprise, he had wished her goodnight – and left! A gentleman, on top of everything! Leaving her utterly confused and frustrated at the door, gazing after him long after he had gone.

She had tried sleeping, but it had not really been on the agenda for her that night. She tossed and turned in her bed, alternately in seventh heaven thinking about Sebastian and their evening together, and in the deepest well of frustration with the jangle of emotions inside her. It would never work, her serious mind had kept telling her all night. She lived in Finland and he in Ireland. He was perfect and she was not. But she wanted to see him so much! A work/holiday fling, Hanna had settled with herself, she could have that… He had promised to call her again soon, and she wondered what his "soon" meant. If Sebastian had asked to come in, Hanna would have invited him in with open arms. But he had not.

What did that mean? That he was the true gentleman she thought him to be? Or maybe he just wasn't that keen on her after all – a possibility that created terror in Hanna's heart. She had felt that Sebastian was pretty much as smitten as her – but then again, it was hard to tell, as she had not really had all her mental faculties working properly.

Hanna felt that the Pandora's box of emotions she had opened since meeting Sebastian was only the beginning... She – always a truly sensible character, logical, eternal planner, always thinking before acting – was ruined.

*So much for that*. Hanna felt as if she had been infected with a terminal disease of never-ending emotional turmoil. *Maybe it's just Ireland getting under my skin*, she reasoned with herself. The Irish did have a gift for high drama. Wasn't there a stone somewhere in Ireland that one could kiss and forever afterwards be a storyteller to beat the band? There was definitely something left of the mystical Celts even in today's Ireland – and whatever it was, it was now utterly ruining her Finnish good sense. That was it: it was all Ireland's fault.

Cheered by the logical conclusion she had managed to draw out of her mangled brain, Hanna went into the kitchen to put on the coffee maker. Sofia would be here soon, and then she'd be able to spend the day analysing Sebastian's every look, word, gesture and kiss. For the hundredth time.

*

'Sofia, here you are, at last! What took you so long? I'm dying here!' Hanna gushed in her fast Turku dialect, yanking the front door open as soon as she heard a knock on the door.

'Now, now. I got here in a super-fast 52 minutes, and it's still only – let's see, 8.09 a.m. on a Saturday morning. I've never seen you up so early before. What is happening to you? This guy must really be amazing.' Sofia threw the comment over her shoulder as she marched purposefully into the kitchen, having first left her mud-caked stable shoes outside the front door. She was kitted out in her work clothes: she owned her own stables at the foot of the Dublin mountains.

Sofia never did anything without looking as if it was the only right thing it was possible to do. She always acted with utter confidence and poise, and it showed in even the smallest thing, like marching into a kitchen. Combined with her startlingly good looks and über-fit body, this characteristic left most men terrified of her, but completely fascinated. Women typically were thrown into the deepest pit of jealousy, and she found she didn't actually have very many female friends – not that she had any time for unnecessary socialising.

'Are you ready?' said Hanna. 'It's finally happened: I'm in love. And I'm going crazy! I don't want to be in love. It's the most terrifying thing I've ever felt. My mind is fried. It'll never work, he's too perfect.'

'Wow, this is big.' Sofia offered her cup for a second helping of coffee.

'Yeah, major big. He seems to be into me too – at least he loved kissing me all evening long, if that's anything to go by. And can you believe it – he didn't ask to come in, or to stay the night. Is that good? Does that mean he respects me, and wants to see me again, or does it mean he doesn't care? What do you think?' Hanna was getting agitated now, her sleep deprivation catching up with her.

'Whoa, slow down, filly. Who is this guy, and where did you meet him?' Sofia was shocked by the state of Hanna: she was always very calm and quiet, but now looked as if she was ready to climb the walls.

'He's gorgeous! His name is Sebastian O'Reilly, he gives personal development speeches and I met him last week at an event of his. Micheál dragged me down to it, and then he introduced us. He's amazing, and...'

'*The* Sebastian O'Reilly? But he's famous. Is it really him?' Even the ever-cool-Sofia was starting to show some signs of excitement.

'Yeah, it's him all right. So he's famous: I never heard of him before. But he is dreamy...'

'You never heard of him? I suppose you've not been here that long yet – I forget at times. He's very well known in Ireland. Everyone would know his face – he's on the telly a lot. Nice speaker, interesting ideas. I've always liked him. So you've fallen for him? And you think he's interested in you too?' Sofia asked.

‘Well, he certainly wasn’t holding back last night. Until we got to my doorstep, that is. But what does that mean? Why didn’t he ask to come in?’ Hanna was off again, worrying.

‘Calm down, the Irish are very traditional. I think it’s a good sign, as –’

‘Do you?’ Hanna jumped in, fiddling with her hair nervously. ‘Oh, I hope so. And he said he’ll ring me again very soon, but when is that? What time is it now? Only half past eight in the morning! Do you think I can ring him now? I just can’t wait for him to ring me.’

‘Hanna. Sit down and relax. Drink your coffee. No, have another sip – good. Now one more. Take a deep breath. OK, that’s better. Tell me everything about him and your date last night.’ Sofia couldn’t get over the way Hanna was embarrassing herself by behaving so out of character. Hopefully when she got it all out, she’d calm down a bit.

Hanna didn’t need to be asked twice. She was away again, and any scrap of calmness that Sofia had managed momentarily to instil in her was out the window. Sofia was shaking her head in amazement. Love was a dangerous business, if this was what happened after one date. Hanna recounted their night in minute detail, coming up for air only an hour later.

‘Wow. He sounds serious.’ Sofia delivered her final judgement.

'Do you really think so? I don't know. Oh, I think I'm totally in love. I've never felt like this about anyone before! But how can it be? We've just met! And is there any realistic possibility of the two of us being together, ever? I have to go back to Finland soon... and he lives here... how would it ever work? Argh, I'm going crazy.'

'Hello, hello! Anyone home?' Micheál called from the door. 'Ah, here you are, girls. Lovely to see you again, Sofia.' Micheál found the girls in the kitchen, nursing a cup of Finnish coffee each. Nothing new here – the coffee maker was permanently on in this house. He swiftly kissed Sofia on the cheek and sat down at the kitchen table. Hanna brought him a cup of coffee too, while Micheál quizzed Sofia about the latest news in her horsey world. It was obvious to him that Hanna was bursting with her news, just waiting to get a word in edgeways.

'Right,' Sofia boomed, 'time for me to go and look after the babies. Loads to do today, before tomorrow's lot come in for their next lesson. Hanna, I'll ring you soon to get an update on your interesting situation. Micheál, I'm off. See you soon, I'm sure. Don't let Hanna do anything too stupid, now.' She gave him a stern don't-let-me-down look.

Sofia was half way out of the door before Hanna got a chance to run after her to ask, 'So, you really think he sounds interested?'

‘Yep, sounds like it to me. But ask Micheál what he thinks, I really have to go now.’

‘Oh, OK, I’ll ask him. Thanks!’

‘*Terve.*’ Sofia was already closing her car door.

Sofia was elated after their conversation, truly delighted for her friend. They had met a couple of months ago at the annual Finnish Independence Day party held in Trinity College in December, and they had immediately hit it off.

They were of the same vintage, and although they were from the biggest rival cities in Finland – Hanna from the old capital of Finland, Turku, and Sofia from the new capital, Helsinki – they found it remarkably easy to chat. In Sofia’s opinion, Hanna’s only shortcoming was her terror of horse-riding. At their first meeting, Hanna had assured Sofia that she loved horses, but it wasn’t until later that Sofia realised this meant that Hanna loved to *look* at horses – from a safe distance.

As she drove, Sofia reflected on her own passionate but disastrous love life. She always seemed to be attracted to unavailable men – either actually unavailable, or just emotionally unavailable. In a sense, this state of affairs suited her – she was very busy, and also very contented with her horses. Did she need a man in her life? She wasn’t convinced.

Sofia's parents had bought her the stables and a house ten years ago, out of the guilt of leaving their only child a victim of divorce, forever rendering her an emotionally unstable and damaged person (or so they had thought). At the time of her parents' divorce, Sofia had already been working in Ireland for a number of months for a famous Irish horse jockey and trainer. She had never wanted to do anything else other than work with horses, and had jumped at the opportunity of her own stables. Her parents' marriage had been on the rocks for years prior to the breakdown, so the divorce had brought only relief to her.

Nowadays, her parents got on pretty well. They still had Sofia in common, after all, and since they didn't have to live together any more, they were able to find common ground again about the two things they agreed on: sailing, and Sofia. They were regular visitors to Ireland, often flying out to see her together, and Sofia felt that she saw them more nowadays than she did in the dark teenage years of endless arguments and upset at home. Sofia had had enough of marriage to last a lifetime, and the only proper relationships she believed in were that between an animal and a human. No conflicts there, ever.

Sofia had always been proud of the fact that aside from the initial capital she had received from her parents, she had been able to make her own living. She was a practitioner of natural horsemanship – a growing trend in Ireland and in the world – a movement based on the idea of communicating with the horse, as one might communicate with one's friends, instead of being its master and using force to bend the animal to its rider's will.

Sofia was getting more and more work in the field, giving talks and demonstrations, as well as teaching her own pupils natural horsemanship principles, and riding and management techniques. As a result, she had managed to attract a number of other natural horsemanship practitioners to take up residence in her stables. She was delighted with the state of affairs in her cosy little horsey world. Did she need someone to share it with her? Most definitely not.

*

Hanna spent the afternoon moping around the house with Micheál, whose heroic efforts to distract her from the one thing that she was interested in – Sebastian – had not been entirely successful. By late afternoon even Micheál was starting to look done in, and the levels of energy were running low. Hanna's sleep deprivation didn't help, and she was becoming irritable, when suddenly her mobile phone started ringing.

It was like a bolt of lightning had hit the two of them. Panic reigned. Hanna clutched the phone as if it were a stick of dynamite.

'It's Sebastian,' she gasped, 'What do I do, what do I do?'

'Answer the bloody phone!' howled Micheál, and Hanna was jolted out of her panic to a lower level of hysteria, one in which she could function enough to find the green button.

'Hello?' she said, her voice breathless.

'Hanna? It's Sebastian. How are you?' Sebastian sounded calm and composed. How could he sound so normal, when Hanna's heart had just run the marathon?

'I'm fine, thanks – a bit tired, I didn't sleep very well last night,' Hanna managed to mumble.

'Ah, poor you! I slept pretty well, although it took me quite a while to drop off. I was wondering, though, if you'd be interested in meeting up later this evening? Unless you're too tired, of course...' Sebastian's poise was starting to falter, and Hanna realised that he must be nervous, too. He wanted to see her again, and she was overjoyed.

'I'd love to – I'm not sure if I have the energy to go anywhere, though. Would you like to come round to my place?' Hanna said.

'That sounds great. Shall I call over, let's say, around 7 o'clock. Would that suit?' Sebastian asked, as polite as ever. His velvety voice was so good to hear – although she couldn't wait to hear it live in just a few hours, when she'd also have the benefit of visual effects. And perhaps some other sensory pleasures. *Now, there was a delicious thought...*

'Oh, yes, that's fine. See you then! Bye!' Hanna clicked off her Nokia, and turned to Micheál, her eyes sparkling and her cheeks flushed.

'He rang you!' Rapid nods from Hanna. 'And he wants to see you tonight!' More nods. 'Oh, that's so dreamy, I wish it was me!' Micheál fake-fainted onto the sofa. 'I'm so pleased for you, honey. You deserve the best, and Sebastian O'Reilly is pretty much as good as they come. But now – we have work to do. We need to get you ready for the second date! And we must start with the underwear, as this time he may not be prepared to walk away...' Micheál leaped off the sofa again, his eyes refocusing keenly on the task ahead: unveiling Hanna's true gorgeousness.

*

Hanna was in a state of high excitement as the hour of 7 p.m. drew closer and closer. Micheál had left a few minutes ago, leaving her alone to agonise over the interminable minutes before her Prince Charming arrived. She was wearing a dark red silky figure-hugging dress, her makeup fresh and natural. Her breath caught in her throat with images of Sebastian doing all sort of things to her... images that had been there from the time they had first met, but became sharper as the probability of realising her daydreams became stronger by the minute. The way Sebastian had kissed her last night had promised a lot more, and she was going to burst if the *himo* – lust – in her did not find release.

Eventually, there was a knock on the door, and Hanna turned feverishly towards it. She had been hovering in the hallway for quite a few minutes now so as not to miss a second of time in Sebastian's magnificent company.

Hanna opened the door, and there he was, in all of his gloriousness. He had a smile on his face, but his eyes were dark. She could smell his scent, already familiar to her. Hanna gasped, and their eyes locked for an intense moment. Sebastian took a step inside the door. Hanna was nervous as hell, but unwilling to move away from the door to let him pass her by in the hallway without getting the one thing for which she had been longing for so many agonising hours: Sebastian's kiss. Her expectant face was angled up towards him, and he bent his head down to hers. Her lips were tingling like mad just before his mouth pressed down on hers, and she was startled by the electric shock she received that moment. An array of other emotions, all better than the last one, assaulted her senses.

Hanna wrapped her arms around his neck, silky but firm under her fingers which automatically found the tips of his slightly curling hair, and she kissed him back with all the power of her agonising wait. He felt and tasted so good. His aroma enveloped her. As long as she lived, she'd never forget this particular smell. His flavour was sweet, all soft skin and fresh air. *Delicious*.

This time, she was not willing to give him the option of walking away, and even though he had just arrived, she found herself half-dragging him into the hallway. It seemed to her that Sebastian was struggling with something in his mind for a bit, but then, to her delight, she found that her "victim" was equally willing, almost pushing her into the living room. She pulled down his jacket while moving him further into the room, where the red sofa awaited them.

*Not a moment too soon*, Hanna thought. She couldn't have taken any more stress. The night and day had been too long: she was a nervous wreck from the emotional and hormonal trauma. Her heart was beating so fast she could hear it in her ears. Could he hear it, too?

Sebastian's kisses travelled down her neck and Hanna found herself gasping for air as she frantically tried to open the buttons of his shirt. Her hands kept slipping, the buttons not co-operating.

'Damn!' Hanna shouted out her frustration.

Sebastian laughed softly, and Hanna heard him mutter the word "feisty". He pushed her down onto the sofa, taking in her silky red dress, the colour of which blended in with the sofa. His eyes roamed over her body as he deftly unbuttoned his shirt.

Hanna's mouth fell open when her eyes caught sight of his smooth chest.

'You're just too good at everything…' Hanna muttered.

'Sorry?' Sebastian asked, his lips now pressed against her collar bone, travelling down towards the inviting dip between her breasts.

Her craving for him was too much to endure, and she moaned aloud. Sebastian groaned, and his hand travelled up her leg, pushing the hem of her dress up, discovering nothing else there above the stockings.

'Wonderful…' his eyes found Hanna's, his dark look accentuating his meaning. *This girl is not shy about showing what she wants*. It was so refreshing. No mind games, no unnecessary bodily coyness. Just pure, simple lust. And she looked so fierce with frustration.

Hanna cried out as his gentle fingers found and began to caress her wetness with ever-increasing tempo. She couldn't wait. He felt so good on top of her, and his wonderful scent was only getting better. She had been on fire for far too many days – since they had met – and she came noisily with a powerful shudder. Sebastian brought his hand up to gently press her stomach, feeling the aftershocks under his palm.

Hanna gazed into his eyes in wonderment. His face was so beautiful. The image of it was becoming very dear to her. He looked even better close up, if that was possible. Who was this godlike creature that had just performed some kind of wonderful magic on her? Yet she wasn't satisfied – as the raw edge of her torment was blunted, so her focus sharpened, and she forcefully pulled Sebastian down to her. The message was clear. Sebastian hastily pulled the rest of his clothes off, and sought her final approval before moving in. She looked almost cross with him, too impatient to wait any longer. Sebastian chuckled again. *This girl is something else*, he thought, slipped on a condom and pushed into her, Hanna aiding him with all her strength. They moved in unison, and forcefully danced their passion to a glorious climax.

Spent, they lay quietly together for a while, enjoying each other's warmth. Hanna rolled herself on to Sebastian's bare chest and gazed down at him. A contented smile spread on her face as she surveyed the man that was becoming so important to her so quickly. It wasn't such a scary thought now, when she was with him. She just felt peaceful. All was well.

'Hello,' Hanna managed.

'Hello there, you beautiful witch,' came his reply. His hand drew circles on her arm, as if he couldn't stop touching her. It felt heavenly, and Hanna sighed contently. She dropped small kisses on his chest. Deliciously soft, almost feminine. He was very delicate, in a masculine way. Nothing rough about him. All his movements were graceful, calm.

The tension she had felt since they met had been too much for Hanna. At last, she was able to relax. She was *tyydytetty* – satisfied.

Sebastian stroked her hair as she listened to his gradually steadying heart rate, her ear pressed to his chest. She loved the feeling of him underneath her – the smoothness of his skin, the heat from his body. She admired the difference in their skin tones, her hand so dark against his white chest. Everything was beautiful about this man. Although it was a warm July evening and she was flushed with the exertion of their lovemaking, the heat from his body was like a balm. It had been so long since she had felt a man's body underneath her.

Sebastian had been hoping for a bit of action tonight, but not really daring to expect it. The tension had been building up all week inside him, thoughts of Hanna dominating his mind and his body. He had known that Hanna had wanted him during their first date, her desire all too clear from their long and passionate exchange of kisses. But he couldn't believe his luck that evening when Hanna had blocked his way at the threshold and forcefully demanded a kiss. After his initial hesitation, Sebastian had needed no further invitation, all his gentlemanly ideas abandoned. This girl was seriously hot, and not afraid to demand what she wanted. There had been no need to prolong the physical agony.

Some time later, Hanna remembered that she was, after all, the hostess of the evening, and got up to make them some of the tea she had promised. Sebastian followed her into the kitchen, where he settled down on one of the comfortable lounge chairs around the table. Hanna bustled around the kitchen, pulling cheese, crackers and grapes out of the cupboards, followed by biscuits and chocolate. She had also baked a cake during that stressful afternoon, a *tiikerikakku* – tiger cake – whose middle displayed a dark stripe when cut, imitating the stripes on a tiger.

Hanna smiled broadly at Sebastian, her eyes shining and her cheeks flushed with pleasure, as she brought tea to the table. They settled down to a comfortable munching, and to their surprise found themselves in possession of a great appetite, as the tension and excitement of the past few days abated and they could unwind again.

'How do you say "thank you" in Finnish?' Sebastian asked.

'Oh, it is *kiitos*, which you pronounce like "geedos",' Hanna answered.

'Geedos!'

Very little else had been said since Sebastian's arrival. The silence between them was companionable and appealing, both of them somehow knowing that they didn't need to talk. It had been like that the first time they met. Sebastian in particular was delighted: professionally, he was never quiet, always in motion, forever travelling from one event to another to speak, or jumping around on a stage. To find someone who didn't expect and demand that he talk all the time was like a deep refreshing draught. They had done enough talking last night on their date.

Hunger having been satisfied, Hanna's longing to feel Sebastian's skin on hers grew once more. She took his hand, and pulled him up the stairs. No words were necessary, and Sebastian was yet again enchanted by Hanna's direct, no-pretence way of dealing with matters. She walked him into her bedroom, where she removed her clothes, looking at him expectantly to do the same. She looked almost surprised that he hadn't followed her suit immediately. No coyness, no games. And he happily obliged – who was he to go against her clear wishes? The passion was incredible, Hanna's intense concentration on pleasure such a surprise to him. And they found that these desires continually renewed themselves, time after time. Hanna didn't remember ever feeling so full of lust – but then again, she had never felt such strong feelings for anyone before. The intensity of her orgasms had been something else altogether, and she just couldn't seem to get enough, no matter how many times she had been pleasured.

Eventually, she could take no more of the torturous pleasure, and begged for mercy from Sebastian's skilful fingers.

He finished off the session with a sensual massage, and Hanna drifted off to sleep in a haze of fully satisfied female contentment.

## *Chapter 5*

After their first date and subsequent night of passion, Hanna and Sebastian became nearly inseparable, only apart when Sebastian was out of town giving his speeches and Hanna had not been able to go with him. Every day Hanna woke deeply delighted about having Sebastian in her life. They went everywhere together: restaurants, the cinema, long walks, gallery openings, parties and piano concerts.

Hanna attended as many of Sebastian's speeches as she could, and he always managed to slip in something they had been discussing together that only Hanna understood, as if their private conversations were continuing through his public events. But then, Hanna always felt that Sebastian was only speaking to her, no matter what the speech was supposed to be about. His eyes often wandered in her direction, with a quick, private smile. Hanna felt like a starstruck teenager when she was looking at Sebastian up on the stage, not quite believing that this amazing creature was the same one that kept hanging around her all the time. It was some sort of a miracle.

It was amazing what being smitten with someone was like. The life she had lived before Sebastian seemed to have been played out in black and white, time slipping by without her much noticing it. But when she met Sebastian, it was as if she had truly seen the wonderful world around her for the first time. She lived for the moment, here and now, when she was with Sebastian – and when they were apart, her constant daydreaming about him still brought a spring to her step.

Her colleagues in the National Concert Hall had noted the big change in her. Nowadays, she was always up for a chat and a laugh, while before she had been very focused on her work and had kept socialising with her colleagues to a minimum. They teased her mercilessly about Sebastian, congratulating her on catching “the most eligible bachelor in Ireland”. She always protested strongly that they were just having fun, since she was going back to Finland soon – but deep down, she was pleased with their words, and she didn’t mind the teasing. She loved hearing his name mentioned.

Hanna’s world view was also changing and opening up. Their constant discussions about the nature of the human inner world, beliefs and values, personal power or definitions of happiness, and the other topics that Sebastian covered, were having a big impact on Hanna’s life. She was seeing everything so differently now. They seemed to be communicating at the level of vibration, of mind harmonies rather than words. It was as if her adoration of Sebastian made it possible for her to have a direct link with his brain and his heart, providing an instant download of whatever he was turning around in his mind as well as what he was feeling.

The concept of telepathy often came to Sebastian when he considered how easily he and Hanna grasped each other's thoughts – apart from the occasional cultural misunderstanding. More often than not, they were able to just laugh those moments away, only occasionally having to suffer a short period of discomfort, when one or the other had his or her nose out of joint. And Sebastian was so pleased that Hanna was able to understand him and the workings of his mind so easily, especially considering that she didn't come from an English-speaking background. Perhaps at some level, it was an advantage, since she always thought about what everyone said very carefully, always on the lookout to learn new words. What Sebastian spoke about was very much like a new language, but most people didn't seem to realise that it needed to be treated as such, all his words needing to be given careful consideration as to their precise meaning.

*

Hanna was at home, packing. She was excited. Sebastian had a speaking engagement in the southwest of Northern Ireland near the border, in Enniskillen, where the magnificent 18th century country house Castle Coole was located. Unusually, the speech had been organised in conjunction with a piano concert as part of an arts festival. When he had heard about this, Sebastian had pulled out all the stops to arrange for Hanna to be the tuner for the concert grand piano they had in the castle.

At home in Finland, Hanna used to do a bit of other concert work outside Helsinki, but she had not yet had an opportunity during her Irish trip to venture beyond the capital for work, and she was very excited. Hanna always enjoyed working in the inevitably wonderful buildings where classical concerts were staged, and she could feel that Castle Coole was not going to disappoint her. She had a passion for architecture and building design, and the old manor and mansion houses littered around Ireland impressed her deeply; she had visited quite a few of them during her first year abroad. She hadn't been to any yet in Northern Ireland, and was looking forward to her weekend away.

Sebastian picked her up on a gloriously sunny Friday morning in early August and they set off to Enniskillen. Their route snaked through many beautiful Irish towns and villages. Hanna had often thought that in Ireland, one was compelled to sightsee on the way to one's destination, as the little roads – many of which were supposedly major national roads – forced the visitor to take in literally every tiny hamlet along the way. Hanna was looking forward to the drive. Part of the fun, she thought, was stopping for an ice cream or a drink in some of the more picturesque spots. In her native Finland, where practically every city, town and village was bypassed, the traveller could only ever admire nature along the motorways – which meant the monotony of vast, evergreen forests.

Having left nice and early, they were not under pressure to get there and so were able to enjoy a leisurely drive. It must have been the best summer on record, as it had hardly rained at all, and when it had, it was refreshing rather than torrential. The sunshine further lifted their mood. Hanna entertained Sebastian with traditional Finnish songs, selecting some upbeat tunes (rather the exception than the rule for Finnish folk-music, which mostly consisted of songs about deep feelings of longing and loss). Sebastian sang along cheerfully, without knowing a word or a tune, and the kilometres flew by.

They arrived at Castle Coole in the early afternoon, and Hanna got to work in the beautiful Great Hall. The piano was an old Steinway grand, and it soon became evident to Hanna that it had not been touched by a tuner for quite some time. She found herself very busy, trying to get everything done within the always-too-small time slot she had been given. Her real job title was piano technician, which meant that she had been trained in all aspects of piano work, not just tuning – although she normally called herself a piano tuner, since that was the title most people understood. Tuning only focuses on the pitch and harmony of the strings, but there was so much more to a piano than that. Hanna had completed part of her training in the Kawai piano factory in Japan. There, she had truly learned the art of perfectionism, as Japanese piano technicians would not let anything go unless it was done millimetre-perfectly.

Hanna was deep in concentration working on regulating the piano action when Sebastian came in from a walk round the beautiful castle grounds.

'Hey, gorgeous – would you like to take a break and look around the house? I've been here before, and I know quite a bit about the history. You've got to see the State Bedroom, which was prepared for King George IV.' Sebastian's presence was like a breath of fresh air, Hanna thought, and felt herself go warm and fuzzy inside. His endearment also felt good. He had this effect on her every time he showed up, and although she had been seeing him now for a month, she still marvelled at it.

Sebastian took Hanna by the hand and lifted her to her feet, rotating her away from the piano for a quick kiss and a cuddle.

'Now, let me be your tour guide for the day, ma'am. Come right this way!' Sebastian got into the character of a North American tourist guide.

'Stop, you silly,' Hanna scolded.

'Now now, bit of culture never hurt anyone,' Sebastian retorted.

Hanna's laughter echoed through the fine stone staircase up to the first floor and into the King's bedroom. She eyed the small bed lustily, before realising that there was no chance she could have a tumble in it with Sebastian. She was losing it!

*

*Sebastian is just so amazing*, Hanna thought, as she watched Sebastian begin his speech to the well-dressed audience. The pianist had played some beautiful Chopin pieces to set the mood, and Sebastian slipped smoothly into full flow. Hanna had to remind herself to actually listen rather than just spend all her time being googly-eyed about him. What is he saying now?

'None of you lack any motivation. You are all completely 100% motivated, at all times. You are motivated *toward* that which you *perceive* to be joyful, and *away from* what you *perceive* to be painful. It's as simple as that...'

Hanna could relate to that so well. She was constantly motivated towards Sebastian, no matter what was happening in her life. Pain was not having him in her life. Pain was considering the lonely future waiting for her in Finland. And it all felt so simple, as long as Sebastian wanted to hang around with her.

After some minutes, Sebastian paused to survey the audience. He was feeling relaxed now: he had felt the usual nervous anticipation in his gut a few minutes ago, just as he always did before a speech. All of his senses had sharpened, getting ready for the performance. His first love in his business had always been getting up in front of a live audience. He never quite knew what would happen and it was exciting. His speech could totally bomb or it could be great – normally it was the latter. Sebastian had been speaking for so many years now that he intuitively understood the rhythm of a good performance: when to pause, when to quicken the pace, when to let rip. He loved it all: the attention of so many people hanging on his every word, not wanting to miss anything, the buzz in the room, the mere fact that he had been given the opportunity to share his knowledge. He sometimes thought of himself as a modern-day preacher, sharing the word of God – or at least, a new and exciting interpretation of the same old story.

His current audience were deep in thought. He could always spot the sceptics a mile away. Then there were the ones that already knew and were simply enjoying the event. But most people tonight were first-timers to the information, evident from the deep frowns and look of concentration on their faces.

And there was Hanna, looking up at him with such intense adoration on her beautiful face. Sebastian's heart expanded at the sight of her. He wanted her in every way possible. And he was delighted that he had time: Hanna was due to stay in Ireland for another five months yet. He would make that time the most wonderful of her life, making sure she wanted to be with him as much as he wanted to be with her... and at the end of it, before she had to decide to go back to Finland, he would declare his intentions.

Sebastian could see that some members of the audience were starting to wonder about the unexpectedly prolonged silence.

He had to stop spending all his time focusing on Hanna and give his audience what they paid for.

'Did everyone have sufficient time to process what I've been speaking about so far? Excellent. You are always motivated, either towards happiness or away from pain. For example, if you'd like to write a book, but somehow believe it to be a painful experience, it is going to be very hard going. Perhaps the pain you associate with it is a fear about not being good enough to actually write it. Or perhaps the assumed pain is connected with you believing that you will be rejected by a publisher. Now, if you believed any of these things, would you write a book? No way: too painful! Remember, we will avoid pain at all costs. So in order to write a book, you must first find any limiting beliefs, and transform them. They can be very small and subtle, sometimes even seeming irrelevant. But if your desire is to be a writer, you cannot believe that writing a book is painful. If you do believe so, you'll never write that book, guaranteed.'

Sebastian could see that there were at least a few aspiring writers in the audience, from the way that they suddenly straightened up in their seats and took notice. It always surprised him how much people relied on examples to illustrate the theories.

'The good news is that you can transform your limiting beliefs. They're just things you picked up along the way, things that you heard or repeated enough times to start believing them.

Nothing has any inbuilt meaning to it; you assign the meaning to everything. So you truly get to choose for yourself. Life lived to the fullest is a life where you follow your *highest excitement* from moment to moment.'

He could so relate to that now, ever since meeting Hanna. He was so excited all the time, thinking about Hanna and the wonderful things he wanted to do with her, or to say to her, or…

'Understanding the direction of your motivation will also make you a better judge of your own feelings. We often confuse anxiousness with excitement. The former is associated with being motivated away from pain. The latter, excitement, is the one you're after: excitement is the key to unlocking everything you have ever wanted. Ask yourself: what excites me right now the most of all the available options? Answering this question will give you an idea of what you really would prefer. If you find that you can't allow yourself to go with your preferred option, the one that seems like the most exciting one, you'll know at once that you have a negative belief lurking in there somewhere. And finding these nasty little buggers that are slowing you down can be great fun, as your life begins to transform immediately in front of your eyes.'

*Like thinking that freedom means no meaningful relationship*. He felt so free with Hanna, it was just amazing! He gave her another smouldering look, a promise of his excitement later that evening. Hanna blushed prettily. So did the woman beside her.

'Everything you want is waiting just there, beyond your immediate viewpoint. You have everything you need to create more. You have the guidance inside you: the emotion of excitement is your guide to everything you want.

'Thank you for your attention. You've been a great audience. I'll take some questions now, and then hopefully we can hear some more beautiful music to finish off this great evening.'

Sebastian finished up with a great big bow and the audience responded by clapping enthusiastically. Hanna was speechless with pride. *He's with me*, she couldn't help thinking, looking around at all the people that were *not with him*!

When the last notes of the piano had died down and the audience had dispersed, Sebastian and Hanna took another walk. It was dark, but the moon was bright and it showed them the way up towards the forest. They sat down on some well-placed rocks, still warm from the day's sunshine.

'Hanna?'

'Yes?'

'I'd like to give you something. But before I do, a little bit of background: I've always been fascinated with the ancient Irish and their Celtic beliefs from the time before Christianity. They had it so right so often, and I feel a great connection to them. Perhaps I sense it through my bloodlines, or perhaps it's only at a conceptual level, but it is there, nevertheless. There is an expression that describes well what I feel when I'm with you. Here – please read this.'

Hanna opened the little green book Sebastian offered her with trembling hands, and took the flashlight he had brought with him. She read out loud, her voice trembling with emotion.

'*Anam Cara*. The ancient Celts believed that when two people were open and trusting with each other, their two souls would flow into each other and be connected as *Anam Cara*, or Soul Friends. This special bond would manifest itself with total acceptance of the other as they are, and aid the Soul Friends in connecting with the mysteries of life.'

Hanna could feel her eyes welling up. *Soul friends*. All Hanna could do was hold Sebastian very tightly, and whisper the magical new words she had learned: *Anam Cara*.

## *Chapter 6*

'Where have you been, you naughty little girl? I haven't seen or heard from you for ages! Or for a day, at least,' Micheál exclaimed as he walked into Hanna's hallway.

'Oh, you know – just busy with the man you hooked me up with,' Hanna said coyly. She was always looking for another ear to fill with her feverish Sebastian-talk, and Micheál was just the man, as he was equally bursting to hear everything.

'Where is he today?' Micheál asked. 'I'm surprised to find you here at home, abandoned by your Prince Charming.'

'Oh, he's gone to a three-day "Change Your Mind, Change Your Life" seminar in Limerick. With his PA Cathy,' Hanna said, the sunshine leaving her face.

'Oh, what's wrong, darling?' Micheál immediately picked up on Hanna's mood change. 'Is Cathy a problem? I think I remember her from the seminar we went to see – she was the one that kept running around organising everything. Tall and slim blondie, superb makeup and hair, if I remember correctly. Tell me everything!' Micheál plopped himself down on Hanna's sofa, settling in for a good gossip session.

'Slim and well-groomed is right – she always makes me feel really frumpy and fat. She's this super-talented British lady he hired a few years ago to arrange his schedule and PR. She used to work in the city in London, and she's so efficient. I think she got converted to this personal development stuff a few years ago, and wanted to get her claws into a new up-and-coming talent. She saw Sebastian at a seminar, and I think decided that she had found the man she had been looking for. Sebastian thinks that she's the real reason why he is as well-known as he is today – he says nobody would know about him if it wasn't for her. He is always singing her praises, but I don't like her one bit, and I think it's mutual. Every time I see her she's really haughty and frosty with me. She looks at me as if I'm some sort of nasty bug that should be squashed. And she covers it all up with a terrible fake smile. Sebastian doesn't see this, of course, as he thinks Cathy is marvellous, but I think she's just a seriously nasty piece of work!' Hanna gushed out all her insecurity and resentment in one breath. She felt better, voicing some of the increasingly present unease inside of her. Hanna felt great in Sebastian's company, but when she was on her own, her head was a little merry-go-round of doubt and uncertainty about the whole situation. She tried her very best to ignore it all.

'Slow down, honey! Take a deep breath. A cloud in heaven's sky, then. It rather sounds like this bitch has a thing for Sebastian – but it doesn't sound to me as if her feelings are returned.' Micheál was firm. *So unlike Hanna to speak about anything for so long in one go: this Cathy has really rubbed her up the wrong way*, he thought privately.

'Do you think so? I didn't think Sebastian liked her that way – but I'm just not sure. And I don't like the fact that she's always ringing him at all hours and booking him to go off to events far, far away, as if to make sure he can't spend so much time with me,' Hanna continued. *And there is nothing I can say to him about this, since I don't have any actual claim over him. And I'll be gone in a few months…* the now familiar sense of dread took over again.

'Well, it can't be easy for her to see you just show up out of nowhere and take her man away from her. She must have been after him for quite a few years. But I don't think you have anything to worry about. I mean, Sebastian would have gone for her years ago if he had any feelings for her. And it *is* his work, darling, to go and speak at all kinds of events all over the place, that's how he makes his living. You can't resent him for that.' Micheál was trying to be diplomatic.

'Yeah, I suppose so – but it's very hard to be parted from him. I haven't seen him for a full day now! And I won't see him until the day after tomorrow.' Hanna moaned.

'Ah, young love!'

'Well, he hasn't actually told me that he loves me,' admitted Hanna.

'Has he not? He must just be shy, or waiting for the perfect moment. It's so obvious that he does love you!' said Micheál.

‘Do you think so?’ *I really am not sure. He’s too perfect for me. I can’t trust it.*

‘Yes, of course! But have you told him how you feel?’

‘Well, no... I think we are both sort of waiting for something. I know he cares for me, and he’d be crazy not to realise that I love him; but he hasn’t said the magic words, and neither have I. I just can’t. I mean, I don’t know what is going to happen when I have to go back to Finland. Maybe I’m just a sort of “summer fling” to him...’

‘I doubt that. Most likely, he just thinks he has lots of time, since you’re not going back for many months yet... I mean, that’s how I feel, too. I don’t want you to go back, I’ll miss you too much!’

‘Ah, Micheál, I’ll miss you too. But I’ll have to go back, although I’m rapidly starting not to want to... my life in Ireland is too perfect.’ *But what must be done, must be done*, Hanna thought grimly.

‘Yes, it is really, isn’t it? I wish my prince would hurry up and get here soon, too!’ Micheál sighed. ‘I’d love to have someone pining for me to come home. And you are becoming totally useless as a friend. Since you’ve run off with Mr Perfect, I never see you any more.’

‘Well, you only have yourself and your wicked matchmaking skills to blame!’ retorted Hanna.

*

‘Quite the famous girl now, Hanna,’ Sofia exclaimed as she walked in. She was waving ‘Image’ magazine at Hanna as she sat down at Hanna’s kitchen table, indicating with the other hand that she wanted coffee. Sofia never did just one thing if she could do three at the same time. Efficiency before anything else.

‘Oh, yes, that thing,’ said Hanna awkwardly, getting the coffee going. ‘Sebastian was invited to a TV awards ceremony and there were photographers there. I never thought the pictures would end up in a magazine! I look awful – Sebastian looks as good as ever.’

‘You look great. Why would you think that?’

‘No, I look awful. But never mind. How did *you* hear about it? I didn’t think of you as the magazine-buying type. You never have a minute of time for anything frivolous.’

‘No, I’ve never bought it before but Micheál rang me – naturally, to inform me of the latest developments in the Hanna and Sebastian saga,’ Sofia laughed.

‘I should have known. That interfering little... but I can’t really be angry with him, given he introduced me to Sebastian!’ The usual dreamy smile was back on Hanna’s face.

Sofia was starting to think that there must be something to this whole falling-in-love business – other than heartache, which was the part she could most vividly remember from her own disastrous attempts at it. Looking at Hanna, it had a lot to recommend it, if it made one glow like that.

'But how are *you* doing?' Hanna asked. She must really make an effort to be interested in other things in the world apart from Sebastian. The topic was messing with her system too much, anyhow. One minute she was up in the clouds, the next in the deepest doldrums. She suddenly recalled a friend of hers from primary school who received a cat for her birthday. From then onwards, every sentence out of her mouth included something to do with the cat, and before too long she found herself without friends. With all her carry-on, Hanna risked losing her friends as well as Sebastian. Not a good thought.

'Great. All is going really well in my life.' Sofia took a sip of the coffee Hanna had just put in front of her. The proper Finnish blend, of course. 'I'm giving another natural horsemanship seminar this coming weekend, and I have people coming to it from as far as Australia. My ads on YouTube are really paying off.'

'Wow, I didn't know you were becoming so famous in the horse circles,' Hanna said. She wasn't that interested in all the horsey stuff, but she admired her friend's passion. It was good to be able to work in the field of one's choosing. *And Sofia's work is not so different from what I do*, she mused. Her pianos also needed to be convinced nicely that they wanted to be tuned. As piano strings are under so much pressure, they really don't want to move. To change the balance of the entire system of tension, Hanna often felt that she was using as much mental persuasion as physical force.

'Sebastian might enjoy one of your seminars,' Hanna thought aloud. 'He's trying to get people to learn to how to be in touch with themselves rather than a horse, but the ideas are similar. It's all very interesting. Can you believe, he has started to use the term "fine-tuning" since he began going out with me? Now he's telling everyone to "fine–tune" their connection to themselves. Isn't he adorable?' Too late, Hanna remembered that she had only just promised herself to be more considerate of other people's interests, and not talk about Sebastian all the time.

'It's so funny looking at you, so in love,' Sofia said.

Hanna cringed inwardly. She was in love all right, desperately. Yet she'd had a growing bad feeling about the whole situation for a while now. Sebastian was starting to take over her whole life. And she didn't know how to stop it. Was it real? Or was he just entertaining himself, since he knew that she was going back home soon?

'…I'm almost tempted to have another stab at this whole relationship-with-a-man business again myself,' said Sofia. One of the Aussies coming to listen to Sofia this weekend *had* looked very interesting. He'd contacted her on Facebook and they had got on pretty well during their conversations... perhaps the love bug was contagious.

'It was totally unexpected, finding Sebastian.' *I still don't believe it's real, any of it.* 'Perhaps Micheál could find someone for you also, since he seems to be such a perfect matchmaker?' Hanna suggested.

'I think not. I have the perfect relationship with my lovely horses, and I don't need a man to interfere with my life.' *Aussie or otherwise*, Sofia thought to herself.

'Sebastian has asked me to go and visit his parents this weekend. I'm so nervous – what if they don't like me?' *Terrified out of my wits is more accurate. It's going to be a disaster, I just know it. I should try to cancel. I can't handle the stress.*

'Nonsense. They are very lucky to have you – they are the privileged ones, not you. A proper Finn as their potential daughter-in-law – what could be better?'

Hanna chuckled at Sofia's patriotism. Sometimes Hanna wondered why her friend lived in Ireland, when so often it was obvious that for her, the country could never match up to her native land.

## *Chapter 7*

'Listen to this, Hanna. I'm writing my new speech for next week's dinner for the German Chamber of Commerce. What do you think?' Sebastian was lounging on the sofa in his Rathgar apartment while Hanna made tea – the Irish way, Barry's Gold Blend tealeaves, and they were even brewed in a proper silver teapot.

'OK, just give me a minute – I can't really hear you in here.' Hanna brought the tea, cups and a few teacakes into the sitting room. 'Now, shoot!'

'Ladies and gentlemen, and blah, blah, blah... tonight I'll be sharing with you how to fine-tune your business by fine-tuning your beliefs. Our beliefs are the hidden Directors of our companies. Learning how to find these hidden bosses, and how to change those that no longer serve us, will make your quarterly financial statement much more pleasant reading,' Sebastian began.

'You are so funny with this "fine-tuning" business! You're putting it everywhere, since I explained how it's done on a piano,' Hanna laughed. His boyish enthusiasm for his grand theories was so engaging. His dark eyes would open up fully and sparkle with his eagerness to make Hanna understand everything he was saying. She loved him so.

'But of course I use it everywhere. I was so fascinated to hear about how you actually tune a piano. It sounded so difficult:

fifths are wide and fourths are narrow; don't tune the intervals exactly flat or you can't play in the 12 different keys – these words are so mysterious to me.'

'If they are such a mystery, how can you even remember what I said? And fourths are wide, fifths are narrow, silly.' Hanna was impressed. Sebastian had such an ability to absorb words, even the ones that made no sense to him, and would lock things away in his mind until he managed to decipher them. He was so perfect. He would have made a great detective – appropriate given his fondness for Agatha Christie's Poirot, who could solve an entire case by adding up the tiniest and most insignificant-looking details.

'I've been playing these words in my mind over and over again since you told me, trying to understand the message contained within them, and I think I've finally got it. Our beliefs also have to be fine-tuned in such a fashion, to allow them to play in perfect harmony with each other. Also, your system of beliefs cannot be too rigid, or otherwise you won't be able to understand those of other people, and that's such a vital skill just for living in society with others.' Sebastian was in heaven.

'Wow, you are something else – everything you hear can be used somehow to explain an aspect of your beloved theories,' Hanna marvelled. She loved the way he kept pulling at his hair when highly excited. Its natural wave emerged, and her eyes followed the curve admiringly.

'These are not mere theories, Hanna: they explain the mysteries of our physical life and beyond. They explain how we can truly be the masters of our own lives, how to change their direction. This is why I like to keep my "Miracles List" with me at all times.'

'Yes, you've mentioned this before. What was that all about?' Hanna's fingers had found the wavy hair and she loved the silky feel of it. A man's hair should not feel so good. It was unfair! Perfection was Sebastian.

'A "Miracles List" is your personal record of all the miraculous things that have happened in your own life. Mine reminds me of the simple truth that physical life is a journey of self-exploration. Everything around you reflects your belief system, and by looking at that reflection, you can learn so much about yourself. My "miracles" remind me that it is all just a question of fine-tuning my ability to be myself. And all will be well.'

'I wish I could understand even half of what you say,' complained Hanna. 'Miracles? What miracles? And if I've got this right, what you are always saying is that I should just be happy and all will be well? That nothing bad is ever going to happen to me ever again?'

'Happiness is the key, yes – but we cannot truly be happy when we carry around with us beliefs that don't belong to us, like a heavy sack of potatoes. I say, drop the potatoes, one by one, and see how your load is lightened. Does a five-year-old child carry on like the weight of the world is on his or her shoulders? No! Children have not yet un-learned the truth – that life is about following your passion in the moment, whatever that may be. A child will only focus on here and now, and think about the next most exciting thing to do – and then go and do it. When do we ever do that as adults?'

'But we have responsibilities,' said Hanna. 'We have to go to work to earn our living so that we can feed and clothe ourselves, and keep a roof over our heads. I'd love to just do the things I want to, but I'm afraid the consequences will be dire.' Hanna was half-serious, half-teasing.

'But when you see someone who really likes their job, doesn't his or her life seem to be a lot easier – and don't they get most things they want a lot easier? And what is the number one desire of all adults? To be happy. We crave happiness, and yet we are afraid of it.'

'If I just did what I wanted to do,' Hanna pointed out, 'I probably wouldn't get up in the morning and go to work. I'd just stay at home.' *Or crawl into your bed and never get out of it.*

'For a few days, maybe. But then you would get bored, which is not happiness. Then you would start to think that you would actually prefer to go to work, or to go somewhere to do something you love. A lot of us actually like our jobs: they create a sense of belonging and happiness, and it is good to be doing something purposeful. Difficulty and complication is self-inflicted – and so it can be self-healed, if we put our minds to it. That is the beauty of the system of life here on this planet – it is supposed to be simple and to feel good. If that is not our experience, then we are unnecessarily complicating matters. We do not trust ourselves.' Sebastian was in paradise.

'Oh, come here, you adorable little philosopher. I actually do like my job, but I'll show you what I find truly exciting at this moment...' Hanna found a way to stop Sebastian's fine-tuning operation.

Other useful life skills thus honed and practised, Sebastian's head shot up.

'What's the matter, darling?' Hanna asked.

'My parents! What time is it? We're supposed to be at their house for dinner.' They both jumped up from the sofa in a panic. Hanna managed to locate her mobile under the sofa.

'It's only 7 p.m. – we still have an hour before we are supposed to be there,' Hanna sighed in relief.

'Oh, that's good. I always lose track of time when I'm with you. This would not be the first time I've been late for something because of your wicked witchery.'

‘Go on out of that, you provoked me!’

‘No, you started it,’ teased Sebastian, pulling Hanna towards him. ‘You did *this* to me first… and then I did *this*...’

‘Stop now or we’ll be late for sure.’ Hanna got up to go to the bathroom and tidy herself up. She looked at herself in the mirror. It would not do to show up in Sebastian’s parents’ house looking like *that*!

Underneath the playful banter, she was feeling very nervous, panicky, even. She did not want to do this. They were going to discover that she was a fraud, she was sure of it.

Sebastian’s parents lived only a few minutes’ walk away from their son’s apartment; Hanna had seen the house from the outside before, but had never yet been inside. As they set off, she stole a sneaky look at Sebastian, who was also beginning to look serious. He rarely spoke about his family, apart from mentioning his sisters from time to time. There seemed to be very little communication between them, although Sebastian did phone his mother often for a chat. Hanna sensed there was some sort of conflict between Sebastian and his father. Perhaps tonight would shed some light on the matter.

All too soon, they arrived, and walked up the Victorian steps to the big black front door of the imposing red-brick residence. It was more like an apartment building than a house for a single family, so large it seemed to Hanna. Her own parents’ pretty but modest detached home would fit into Sebastian's parents' mansion many times over, and Hanna couldn't help feeling intimidated. Noticing her discomfort, Sebastian gave her hand a supportive squeeze. Hanna felt a little better, although she quickly dropped his hand once the door started to open. It didn't seem appropriate to be intimately connected to Sebastian – even by the simple gesture of holding hands – while being introduced to his parents. Better to be overcautious.

'Hello, mam,' said Sebastian, leaning over to kiss a petite and well-groomed smiling woman on the cheek. She seemed friendly in a very down-to-earth way, and Hanna, suddenly aware she had been holding her breath, relaxed.

'You are most welcome, Hanna. I'm Eileen. It's lovely to finally meet you.'

Hanna liked her. Sebastian's mother was not snooty, despite her polished appearance, and her welcoming words gave Hanna a sense of true warmth. Eileen moved to greet Hanna in the Irish way with a kiss or two on the cheek. Hanna was still finding this very hard to get used to. She personally felt the proper approach when meeting new people was to smile politely and shake hands from a safe distance – but she extended her cheek as she had learned to do. *When in Rome*... Hanna sighed: one down, one to go.

With her hand on Hanna's arm, Eileen directed Hanna through the magnificent hallway and into the front sitting room, all the while chatting amicably about the weather, asking how she was finding life in Ireland, and other such small talk. If she hadn't been such a pleasant woman, Hanna would have found the physicality of the guidance intimidating. Yet somehow she felt comfortable with Sebastian's mother, and allowed herself to be led through to the dining room, beautifully laid out for dinner for four.

Eileen ushered Hanna towards one of the large couches arranged in the bay window and asked her what she would like to drink. Sebastian came to the rescue, as it was obvious to him that Hanna was feeling tongue-tied. Eileen promptly disappeared through the side door, and Hanna got a breather from her well-meaning attention.

'Your mother is lovely,' she said, turning to Sebastian. 'She is just how I pictured her from your description, although better groomed. And she looks just like you.'

'I take after her, as does my littlest sister – but my other sis is more like my dad.'

'Where is your dad?'

'Ah, just probably in his study finishing up on some work. He'll come down when he's ready.' It was obvious from Sebastian's tone of voice that he was annoyed with his dad for not being there to meet Hanna.

‘He’s some sort of legal person, isn’t he?’ Hanna was trying to remember, through her nerves, what Sebastian had told her about his father’s work.

‘Yeah, a Senior Counsel. He’s pretty high up in the court system, and don’t you know, he knows it very well,’ said Sebastian.

Hanna felt her nervousness escalate. In her mind’s eye she saw her own parents. *They would never have anything in common with these people*, she thought. Now retired, they had both spent long decades working in factories and shipyards, wearing the clichéd blue overalls. Hanna had done so herself for some summer work experience.

Eileen returned to the dining room. ‘Here you are: two glasses of apple juice. I’ll go and call your father now.’ She hummed happily as she disappeared into the hall and up the stairs. *She* was clearly not upset by Sebastian’s dad’s absence. Hanna suspected that it would be difficult to make Sebastian’s mother upset about anything.

Hanna and Sebastian sat in silence, sipping their drinks. Sebastian looked gloomy, and Hanna felt herself growing tenser. It was so unlike him: he was always cheery, just the same as his mother, and seeing him so unhappy was disconcerting. He looked like a little boy whose toys had been taken from him.

'Hello, hello! So here is the mystery woman! Sebastian's been very tight-lipped about you, but I really can't understand why. How do you do? I'm Gerald. But you are gorgeous. It was about time that my son brought home a nice girl. He's getting too old to be single: travelling all over the place, to talk about "positive thinking", of all things.' Sebastian's father turned to his son. 'How many times have I told you to give up all that hippy nonsense and settle down with a proper girl to have a family? Not to mention getting a proper job – one that involves staying here in your home town rather than gallivanting all over the place. A proper job and a proper girl, I tell you: that is the only secret in life you need to know.'

Hanna was taken aback by Gerald's strident voice, and his vehement dismissal of Sebastian's choice of life. He had not spoken the harsh words in a humorous way, even though he'd been smiling, and Hanna could begin to understand why Sebastian didn't visit home much. The rest of Ireland seemed to worship Sebastian's every word, but Sebastian's father was clearly the exception to the rule.

Gerald was a big man, as tall as Sebastian, but more robust around the midsection, and he walked straight up to within an inch or so of Hanna after delivering his opening statement. He pumped Hanna's hand up and down as he bent over to land a big kiss on her cheek, right in the middle of what Hanna most definitely considered her personal space. She never knew which cheek was to be kissed, and there had been a tense moment of duck-and-dive between the two of them. In addition to the intrusion of privacy, she was also uncomfortably aware of having been marked with Gerald's overpowering aftershave, which she knew she would now be smelling all night.

'Nice one, Dad,' said Sebastian grimly. 'Can we just try to get along for one night, without the insults flying all over the place? Please behave.'

'But I always behave in the most impeccable manner in such beautiful company, son. Just making sure we know where I stand on the issue of what's good for you. I intend to keep reminding you until you wise up. Enough about you – Hanna, tell me all about yourself.'

'Dad, leave her alone! She hates being interrogated. Let's just sit down and eat.'

'Yes, sit down, please,' Eileen piped up, without seeming even the slightest bit frazzled by the father-son exchange. *Must be so normal in this house*, Hanna thought. She felt shaken, and was relieved to be able to sit down. Even Gerald seemed to have piped down after his opening bluster, and Hanna was grateful for a few quiet moments. The next battle was sure to begin soon, if she had understood anything about the family dynamics in play, and she prepared herself for a long night.

Everything Sebastian's father said seemed to elicit a deep, disapproving frown from Sebastian at best, and at worst, a long, heated exchange. It was clear that Gerald loved to provoke his son, and Sebastian rose to the bait every time. Hanna had never seen him so annoyed about anything in all the time they had spent together. She sat through three agonising courses of deliciously cooked food before they were all released from the prison of the dining table. Sebastian stomped into the front room, Hanna trailing behind him. They sank down on the large sofa, Sebastian still growling with frustration as Hanna put her hand on his sleeve.

'The circumstances don't matter,' she reminded him. 'Only your own state of being matters.'

'I know, I know! I taught you that. I just don't seem to be able to apply it to my relationship with my dad. Every time I come over here, I resolve to keep my cool – and every time I lose it within seconds. He really knows how to push my buttons. I'm so sorry you had to witness that.'

'Shush, I know, I know,' soothed Hanna. 'It's all right. Dinner is over and we can go home soon. By the way – that was really good food. Your mum is a great cook.'

Sebastian's face softened. 'She's wonderful. It's all down to her that I didn't go mad growing up in this house. Luckily, my dad always worked really hard so he was hardly ever here. And

I'm going to sit down later tonight with my notebook and banish the demons my father has implanted in my mind once and for all.'

'Maybe *much* later,' suggested Hanna. 'I think you'll need some R&R after tonight's experience… We all do.'

'Hmmm…' murmured Sebastian, pulling her closer to him on the sofa. 'Did you have anything particular in mind...?'

'You'll just have to wait and see.'

They survived the rest of the evening – indeed, rather enjoyed it, as Gerald retired to his study after only a brief after-dinner appearance, and they spent a pleasant time chatting with Sebastian's mother. Returning home, Hanna made good on her promise of relaxation, after a bit of high-level cardiovascular exercise. *Who said working out couldn't be highly pleasurable? The girl has some appetite*, Sebastian mused fondly, indulgently playing back their energetic fun and games in his mind. *Hanna is so wonderful.*

But back to work: he'd have to continue his quest to chase the evil spirits out of his mind. Sebastian opened his notebook. He tried to relax, since he knew nothing would happen without him being in the right frame of mind. He had a special section entirely devoted to his relationship with his father. The numerous dated entries showed him that he had tried so hard to find the belief that was responsible for continuing the bad relationship between him and his father. He ran through his mantra in his head: *I know that I exist and I am worthy, and in being so, I know that I have everything I need to create more. I know there is only this one moment, and that there are no expectations on my part; there is only struggle in not being myself. I always have everything I need; I will always have everything I need to create more. I surrender, surrender, surrender. All is well.* As with every time he recited it to himself, Sebastian soaked up the meaning of the words to calm him down, to raise his spirits.

He read through some of his previous entries, in which he had written down a myriad of beliefs that the topic of his father had brought up. *Very fruitful subject*, he noted. He knew it was all about not believing he was not worthy – many negative beliefs were rooted in this – but yet he felt there was something more, something else that he was missing. He still fell down the emotional scale every time he met his dad. *What can't I see? How is it serving me to throw a hissy fit each time I see my dad?* It had to be serving him somehow, or otherwise he wouldn't be doing it to himself, time after time. *What is the alternative that is so much worse than freaking out?* Perhaps he was afraid that his father was right, after all, and that he was no good.

Sebastian sat staring into nothingness for a long time. An image from his childhood appeared in his mind's eye. One summer they had gone on holiday to Sligo, where they had stayed in a smart hotel by the beach, his father sneering at him for being a sissy for not getting into the freezing cold water of the Atlantic, when he himself had just walked straight in. And when Sebastian went to his mother crying, his dad had mocked him again before forcibly dragging him back to the water.

There had been no more crying in front of Daddy ever again after that. And his dad had approved of him more when he fought back, even encouraging it by egging him on. His dad never lost his cool with him; he was above it all, the ultimate authority figure. So confident, and so sure he was always right. Sebastian had always envied him that. He had spent his entire life questioning everything. And his father always madc him feel like shit. He was never good enough for him. And how was *that* supposed to be okay? It hurt him so much that his dad never approved of him fully. He could not relax and be himself in Gerald's presence. He was just a performing monkey, and he could not respect himself.

Sebastian had worked so hard all his life to show everyone that he was brilliant, but his public success didn't get any notice at home. Apparently, getting married and having a family was much better. And Sebastian intended to do that – but he knew that the bar would just be raised higher, and something else would be demanded of him. He was so tired of it all. He got up, closed his book, having written down nothing at all, and went to bed.

## Chapter 8

The buzz in the Sofia's classroom was so high that it was almost visible; her ten students sprawled on comfy sofa chairs, chattering animatedly. Sofia had spent a long time thinking about how to create the most inspiring surroundings for learning. The room had been painted a stimulating shade of new-leaf green, a colour that usually looked drab and uninviting in Ireland, as the light levels were often too low – but Sofia knew that she could get away with it in this space. The ceiling was unusually high, and most of the walls on both sides were of glass, flooding the room with light and bringing the paintwork to life.

Wind chimes created soothing sounds outside, hanging from the eaves of the log cabin in which her classroom was based; the stables were at the other end of the building. She had always wanted to teach, but having begun teaching horse-riding the old-fashioned way, she had gradually become unsatisfied with the traditional methods. When she came across natural horsemanship, she was instantly sold on the ideas behind it, and there had been no turning back.

'OK, class,' roared Sofia. 'Let's listen to me for a while.' This got a great laugh. 'Good morning to you all. I can see you are all bright-eyed and bushy-tailed, and eager for more? Am I right?' More laughter. 'Nothing wrong with your laughing muscles, anyhow. This morning, we are going to discuss the importance of body language when communicating with our horses…'

After the morning session, one of her students approached her. Sofia was busy switching off her computer and projector, and he had to alert her to his presence by softly whistling.

'Oh, I didn't see you there.' Sofia turned around and smiled. It was the Australian. He was so easy on the eye: well-built, tall and tanned, in a very natural way, no doubt a result of working outdoors all his life. His long hair's natural colour was probably brown, but it had been bleached blond by sunlight; it had clearly rarely seen a pair of scissors, and unconsciously he flicked it out of his face.

'This stuff you're teaching us is ace!' gushed the Aussie enthusiastically. There was something special there. He looked... natural. As if the whole civilization thing had somehow passed him by. *A wild Aussie...* thought Sofia dreamily. His whole person exuded an uncomplicated enthusiasm for life. Most people seemed to be weighed down by an entire life's baggage; this man carried no baggage at all. His eager-little-boy manner radiated positive energy, and he looked as if he was up for anything, as long as it was fun.

'I'm really glad you like it, particularly since you came such a long way to attend the course,' Sofia said, politely. *Now, what was his actual name?*

'Yeah, it's all just ripper. I'm Aaron Bailey – bet you didn't remember that.'

Sofia was startled, but his manner was so easy that she couldn't help smiling at him. He was gazing intently at her, and she noticed that his eyes were a sort of murky green – so perfect on him. Everything about him was grounded, earthy, above all human nonsense.

'I was wondering if you might have a job for me here at your place after the course is finished? I've a three-month travelling visa to Ireland, and I'd like to stay the whole time. My ancestors come from here and it would be good fun to get to know the place a bit better. I don't need to be paid much, if anything – I'm really just looking for bed and board, and I can muck in at the stables for you as much as you'd like.'

'Yes, I do believe we could use you here after the course,' said Sofia. *Now, where did that come from?* She had all the help she needed, and another mouth to feed was just another complication. But somehow she knew instantly that she needed him to stay, and his proposal had been just the excuse she was looking for.

*

'Hanna, it's David here. How are you?'

'David, wonderful to hear from you! Everything going OK in Helsinki? Are the Finns behaving themselves?' Hanna was delighted to hear from her colleague, but wondered why he had rung her on her mobile.

'I'm afraid I have some bad news,' David said, with a quiver in his voice. 'My mother has been diagnosed with cancer. The doctors are saying that it's terminal, and she only has a few weeks to live, if that.' It was obvious that he was holding back tears.

'Oh, David, that is terrible! I'm so sorry to hear that!' Hanna was in shock.

'Yes, it is awful. And I'm afraid this means, Hanna, that I'm going to have to come back to Ireland pretty soon.' David sounded grave.

'Of course, yes – I should have realised that straight away! When were you thinking about coming back?' Hanna asked. There was a knot of panic growing in her abdomen, and her chest felt constricted.

'I was actually thinking about the end of this week, if that was to suit you. I'll have to take my holidays then to be with my mother, so perhaps you'd be able to work for another week or so once I return? Have a think about it – my head is all over the place and I can't really think straight. You can stay in my house as long as you stay in Ireland – there are two bedrooms, after all,' David blurted out. He sounded desperately sad, apologetic and frantic all at once.

'Yes, okay,' said Hanna. 'That's very soon – but of course you'll have to come home as soon as possible. I'll see what I can do. Gosh, I thought I'd still have a few more months in Ireland! I'll have to speak with Sebastian also, of course,' Hanna was trying to get her head around it all. This would change everything. Panic was setting in. She had been deliberately not thinking about the day when she'd have to go back to Finland since things were going so well with Sebastian.

'Ah, I'd forgotten about Sebastian. How are you two doing? It seems that the romance is quite serious?' David was attempting to be civil and interested in Hanna's life, which was, like his, unravelling fast.

'Yes, it is pretty serious – but we've never spoken about what happens when I have to move back to Finland. Well, I suppose it is now time for that chat…'

'Poor Hanna. I'm so sorry about all this,' David apologised.

'David, it is not your fault. You have to think about your poor mother now, not me. We'll sort something out with Sebastian,' Hanna assured David. 'I'll phone you later once I've had a good think about what to do. Bye for now.'

'Sure, speak to you then.' David rang off.

*Oh my God*. Hanna was despairing. She had been banking on the next few months to come up with some plan with Sebastian about their future. They had never yet talked about it. One of her ideas, her secret hope, had been that Sebastian would agree to move to Finland, at least for a while, while they figured out how their relationship was going to work. *No time like the present to find out!* She picked up her phone again and dialled Sebastian's office.

'Good afternoon, Sebastian O'Reilly's office,' a bright British voice answered.

'Oh, hi Cathy – is Sebastian around?' Great: just what Hanna did not want to do was to beg snotty Cathy to graciously allow her to speak with Sebastian.

'Hello Hanna, how are you? I'm afraid Sebastian's tied up in a meeting at the moment, but he should be back in the office in about an hour or so. Shall I leave a message for him?'

'Yes – can you ask him to phone me as soon as possible? It is very urgent.' Hanna couldn't prevent the panic from seeping into her voice.

'Oh dear, sounds serious! I hope you're not ill?' Cathy probed. This could be something juicy now – perhaps even the opportunity she had been looking for.

'No, I'm okay. In fact, it's David's mother – David is the piano tuner in Helsinki doing my job at the moment.'

'Yes, Sebastian's mentioned him.'

‘David’s mother has fallen ill and David has to come home early, which means that I’ll have to move back to Finland much sooner than planned,’ Hanna gabbled, relieved to be telling someone, even if it was Cathy. There was something about that woman that made Hanna go rigid all over, as if some unknown threat lurked behind her pleasant features, putting Hanna on her guard all the time.

‘Gosh, that is serious. I’m so sorry. Perhaps you’d better tell Sebastian in person. Could you come into the office in about an hour?’ Cathy suggested, faking a concerned tone as best she could. This was great news: Hanna would be going back to Finland! And not a moment too soon. *Sebastian is way too interested in her*, Cathy thought, feeling the usual irritation overtaking her.

‘Oh, okay, I’ll do that. Yes, it is better not to tell him over the phone. See you then.’ Hanna put down the phone.

Cathy smiled, her irritation replaced by a feeling of hope. *Very interesting*, she thought. Hanna and Sebastian’s relationship had flourished in recent weeks, and it had hurt Cathy more than should be possible. She had always loved Sebastian, from the very first moment that they had met. She had not seen any other option but to convince him to hire her to run his office and PR for him. She had even worked purely on commission in the early days, getting a cut of the fees for the speaking engagements she arranged for him.

Cathy had thrown herself into making Sebastian the success he was today. She had sacrificed all her free time until Sebastian was able to hire her properly and to pay her a full-time salary for the job, but she hadn't cared. She had been able to spend each day with him, and nothing was better than that. Besides, she was excellent at her job, and Sebastian was forever telling her that he couldn't have done it without her. Cathy had waited patiently for many years for Sebastian to notice that she was perfect for him in so many more ways than just work. But the boy was so slow. Sebastian liked Cathy, of that she was sure, but for some reason he had not yet learned to see her in quite the right light.

The healthy eating and the hours Cathy put in at the gym, as well as regular beauty and hair treatments, made sure that she was attractive and fashionably slim. Her wardrobe taste was immaculate. Yet nothing seemed to be enough for him. Cathy had started to doubt her previous conviction that Sebastian was just being very professional, not wanting to ruin their good working relationship by reaching out for her in other, more personal ways. In all the ways that burned Cathy and kept her awake at night.

And then the Scandinavian slut had turned up! Hanna was Sebastian's first proper girlfriend since Cathy had started to work for him. Yes, there had been flings; she had known all about them and had got rid of a girl or two from his life, but he had never seemed too serious about them, so it had not been difficult. But now the unfortunate dalliance with Miss Finland had to end: it was time for the high and mighty Sebastian O'Reilly, who would be nothing without her, to properly recognise her talents.

Here was her opportunity now, and she was determined to make the most of it. She had always succeeded in everything she had set her hard mind to, and she was not going to be defeated. But what would be the right thing to do? What to do to put a spanner in the works of the Sebastian and Hanna love story? The fact that Hanna would have to move back to Finland now, months ahead of the planned time, was indeed great news. All she would have to do was to make sure that once Hanna went back to Finland, all communications between them would stop, and Sebastian's focus would be directed back to where it belonged: Cathy. She knew Sebastian would be gone for at least another hour and half, which should give her all the time she needed to plant a useful idea or two in Hanna's mind. She just had to think of something very clever.

*

'Hanna! Do come in! Sebastian should be back any minute now. Would you like a cup of tea or coffee while you are waiting?' Cathy smiled. She still didn't know what she was going to do, but she trusted her gut instincts to deliver some stroke of genius at the right moment. For now, she would just watch Hanna very carefully, absorb her state of being and plant a seed or two of doubt.

'Oh, thanks. I'll have a coffee, if you don't mind,' Hanna replied. She was feeling edgy, and Cathy was the last person in the world she wanted to be having a chat with. The girl always managed to unnerve her. She was always smiling, but her eyes looked steely, the smile never reaching them. Was she just a typically reserved Englishwoman, or did she truly not like Hanna?

Cathy came back a few minutes later, carrying a cup of coffee and a few biscuits. She was staring at Hanna in a way that was completely freaking her out. Like a cat watching its prey.

'Oh, are you not having any?' Hanna asked, her voice shaky, trying to be polite.

'Oh no, I can't stand tea or coffee in my condition,' Cathy smiled at Hanna meaningfully, placing a hand on her belly. It had come to her in a nanosecond. It was so simple, the oldest trick in the book. Nothing would be as effective, she decided, as making Hanna's Prince Charming look like a common good-time boy and a two-timing bastard. Sebastian had this natural innocence about him that everyone found so endearing, and it would hit Hanna very hard to believe that he was in fact a nasty piece of work, who had been busily going behind her back. Cathy didn't need to fake the sigh of contentment that left her lips.

Hanna looked at Cathy. She seemed very pleased with herself, positively beaming, in fact. *What condition is she talking about?* It took Hanna a few moments to piece it all together. Her mind was so full of her own life drama that it was very hard to concentrate on anyone else's life.

'Oh, are you expecting a baby?' she blurted out.

'Indeed! I'm over the moon – just coming up to three months now.'

Hanna smiled politely. She didn't care about Cathy's baby. She couldn't focus on anything but her own immediate problems. She had to go back to Finland. Her time was up.

'Well, it was nice talking to you – I'll just go and finish the email I was in the middle of when you came in. Sebastian shouldn't be too long now.' Cathy walked into her office, leaving Hanna alone in Sebastian's office. *First seeds planted*, thought Cathy, and high-fived her imaginary double. She was just such a genius! It was a bit of a mad plan, but it had felt like the right thing to say. Sebastian was always going on about how to trust one's instincts and Cathy could agree with him now. She felt so elated. And now she would just observe the events unfold. And she'd know when the moment came to up the ante.

*Imagine – Cathy pregnant*, Hanna thought. Strange to think that Cathy had been pregnant most of the time she had known her, without letting anything slip. Hanna was half-heartedly wondering about who the unlucky daddy was, when Sebastian walked in.

'Hanna! What a wonderful surprise! It's brilliant that you've come to see me. Come here, you.' Sebastian grabbed Hanna into a tight bear-hug. 'You should do this more often. I'd love to spend time with you during the day.' Sebastian was in high spirits.

'Put me down, Sebastian, I have some bad news to tell you,' Hanna warned.

Sebastian was immediately alarmed. 'What is it? Are you hurt?'

'I'm fine. It's David – his mother has been diagnosed with terminal cancer. The doctors say she only has a few weeks to live, so David is going to come home much sooner than planned,' Hanna explained, feeling miserable. She was trying to empty her mind, to keep her world from disappearing. She didn't want to cry. She sat down rigidly, avoiding Sebastian's eyes.

'How soon?' *This is a disaster*, Sebastian thought. And Hanna just sitting there. What was the girl thinking? At times it was impossible to read her! The warning bells were ringing in Sebastian's ears, and he could feel panic rising. If only she would look at him.

'He's going to come back to Dublin this Friday,' Hanna said matter-of-factly, gazing out of the window. She focused her stare far beyond the walls of the office. Her back was straight, her posture wooden.

'But that's not possible! That's too soon. Will you lose your job in the concert hall now?' Sebastian asked, feeling the disaster that was about to utterly change his life knocking at his door. This could not be happening. They were supposed to have many more months of happiness left to them in Ireland before they needed to make any actual decisions about their future. For he truly wanted them to have a future together, in whatever form or place – he could not imagine a life without her.

'Yes, I'll have to move back to Finland next week, and take up my post in Helsinki again, as they won't have a tuner now. It's the best tuner job in Finland. I don't want to lose it,' Hanna said defensively.

*Move back to Finland.* The words chilled Hanna. Her beloved home country – now sounding like a death sentence. Her perfect world was ending.

'Oh. So soon.' Sebastian looked at Hanna, willing her to look at him. What was she thinking? He wanted to scream and demand that Hanna stayed in Ireland. That she would stay with him, have a life with him. Hanna's jaw was set tightly. It was obvious that she had made up her mind, and there was no changing it now. He wanted to grab her by her shoulders and turn her around. Then he might get a better idea of what she was actually thinking, and be able to demand an answer from her to his unsaid question. Had it all just been a bit of fun for her? Did she care for him? It didn't seem so. She was so cold.

'Hanna…'

'Yes?' Hanna continued to be fascinated by what was going on outside of Sebastian's office window. She was desperately trying to hold back her tears. He didn't care for her, it was obvious from his lack of reaction. The only sensible thing to do was to keep her cool and to get out of there as fast as possible, before she lost it. She had told him, and it was time to go. Her short stay in paradise was over. Sebastian was just a dream, unattainable, perfect. Hanna wished with all her heart that she could be enough for him but it was not to be. There was no way she was going to embarrass herself further by begging.

'Hanna…' Sebastian felt suddenly very nervous. He realised that Hanna had never actually told him that she loved him. Did she? It didn't seem that way now. Perhaps he had just been a holiday fling to her. Sebastian wanted to tell her that he loved her, but it didn't seem like the right moment. He didn't want his heart thrown back at him.

'Hanna, do you really have to go?' Sebastian said quietly.

'Well, I have to. Sebastian, you knew this was always on the cards, anyhow. I just have to go back sooner than anticipated.' *Pride kept intact, well done*.

'But…' Sebastian wanted to plead with her. How pointless. It was all over, he could feel it. Like running in quicksand.

'Yes, I really have to go. I can't stay in Ireland,' Hanna explained firmly. 'My life is in Finland.' *Whatever that life is*.

'I've really enjoyed my time here, but let's face it: I've no job or home,' Hanna stated coldly. He was making this a lot worse than she had anticipated. *These Irish, they always wanted to discuss everything for so long*. It was excruciating. They were gluttons for pain. She wanted it over and done with. No point in hanging around any longer. Could he not understand?

'I can't just quit a post like mine,' Hanna repeated. 'There are not many of them to be had. It is the most prestigious of its kind in Finland, and I've been incredibly lucky to get it so young.'

'But we could work it out, somehow, couldn't we?' Sebastian had to do something.

'Make what work?' What was he trying to say? Hanna's heart was beating so fast, she was feeling faint. She had to get out soon or she'd have a mental and a physical breakdown.

'This…' Sebastian didn't know how to continue. What was it that they had? Surely they could make it work? But perhaps he didn't mean so much to her, after all. And she was still not looking at him. He felt horrible.

‘Sebastian, I have to go back to work now. I’ll talk to you later, okay?’ She had to get out, now.

Hanna was off with a quick hug. It was all hurting her too much; she had to go before she destroyed it all by begging him for something he clearly couldn’t give her.

Sebastian could do nothing but let Hanna run out of his office. It felt so final, and a cold shiver ran through him. He had thought that their relationship was going so well, and had been pretty sure that once the day of Hanna’s departure approached, he would have convinced her to stay in Ireland, somehow. Now it seemed that they were forced to make a decision much sooner than anticipated – and Hanna’s reaction had been terrifying.

Was this how she was going to say goodbye?

*

‘Oh, Micheál, it’s awful, I really don’t want to go back to Finland yet! I don’t want to leave Sebastian!’ Hanna was crying on the phone, having related to Micheál the tale of what had happened. She had just about managed to finish her day’s work, and had somehow arrived at home. Outside her front door, she broke down, and stumbled into the hall, not seeing anything through her teary eyes.

‘Hold your horses, you poor thing, I’ll be there in a jiffy!’ Micheál cried. Hanna could hear him rushing around his house.

She was holding onto the phone for dear life. She heard keys jingling, then the bang of the front door and hurried footsteps. As the car engine roared to life, she could hear Micheál repeating to himself, 'Hold your horses, hold your horses!' He kept up a comforting jibber-jabber during his drive over to Hanna's house, until she heard his car outside, and his hurried footsteps towards her door. Shouting into the phone, 'Open the door, open the door', he ran in and enveloped her in a big hug, while Hanna sobbed her eyes out.

Micheál fussed around her like a mother hen. He made her sit down at the kitchen table, blow her nose, wipe her eyes and drink a strong cup of tea. 'Now, chicken – tell me everything.'

'I got such a shock when David rang me. I feel sorry about his mother, but I resent her for messing around with my life like this. Everything was just so perfect, my… thing with Sebastian was going so well, and I was hoping for much more. And then I went to see him today, and it's all over. He doesn't care about me,' Hanna wailed. More tissues were required.

'Okay, now, let's look at this analytically. What exactly did he say?'

'Well, he didn't say much. Nothing really. He just… oh, it was awful. And he let me walk out of there so easily….' Hanna didn't know what to say. It was all too horrible for words.

'And what had you said to him?'

Micheál had a good idea about what had actually happened. He had got used to Hanna adopting a chilly, offhand stance whenever the going got a bit tough. It seemed to be her survival technique, to shut everyone out, and by the looks of it, this included herself. *A little bit Scarlett O'Hara, saying she'll think about something difficult tomorrow*, thought Micheál. He could just picture Hanna rigidly standing in Sebastian's office, probably saying things like, "Nothing I can do, I must go back to Finland", which would sound terrible to a man in love with her. *At least she's open with me*, Micheál thought, his own heart twisting in his chest. It seemed that he was going to lose her too, at least physically, to Finland. Not a nice thought: not at all. But he had to be strong for Hanna now – she needed him. He'd have time to fall to pieces later. Now was not the moment.

'Well, I said to him that they need a tuner pretty quick in the Helsinki concert hall, since David is leaving. Which is true. They'll want me to come back straight away, and I can't leave them in the lurch.' Hanna began crying again.

'Yes, darling, I know that – but did you not think that Sebastian might interpret that as meaning that you don't care about him, and that all you want is to go back to Finland as soon as possible?' Micheál sighed. The girl could be impossible at times. It was perfectly obvious to him that the now-unhappy couple were made for each other.

‘Well, he should know by now that my job is very important to me!’ It seemed that Hanna was willing to defend her position to the bitter end. Which would not make Micheál’s job of reconciliation between the lovebirds easy.

‘Yes, darling, of course it is. But Sebastian needs to feel that he’s important, too. I think you need a moment now to calm down. Let’s watch a bit of telly, and relax on the sofa. Try to put the whole sorry saga out of your head just for a while.’ Micheál knew not to push Hanna any further. *The poor thing has been through the mill already today*, he thought tenderly, his heart aching for her.

Hanna did as she was told, and soon she was fast asleep. Micheál kept stroking her hair, long after she was dead to the world. He was pretty messed up himself: the thought of Hanna going back to Finland was having a terrible effect on him. He had always known it would be difficult to let her go, as their friendship had only deepened as the months of her stay in Ireland had passed. But he couldn’t think about that yet – Hanna still needed him.

Hanna woke up an hour later, and found that Micheál had made them dinner. ‘Oh, you are a star! What would I do without you?’ said Hanna. As the words left her mouth, her face started to crumple again. Micheál saw this and swept her up in a huge hug, murmuring, ‘I know, I know’, and ‘It’s all right’. He directed her to the table, where she started mechanically putting food into her mouth. Anything was better than thinking about what had happened to her to end her perfect life.

*

Cathy knew her moment had come. She had watched in delight as Hanna ran out of Sebastian's office, and it was obvious to her that things had ended badly. It was now or never. She had been keeping an eye on Sebastian for the rest of the day, making a final analysis of what had happened with Hanna, and Cathy was sure she was right. She had never seen him so crushed. Hanna had practically twisted his heart out and left it for the vultures. But Cathy would swoop in and rescue it. It was now or never. Sebastian was finally going to realise the gem that had been sitting right in front of him all these years. All her hard work was finally going to be rewarded with the one thing she wanted the most: Sebastian. Her darling. All hers.

But before she worked on Sebastian, she had to make sure Hanna was completely out of the picture. There had been no further communication between the two today, of that she was pretty sure. It was time to put her little plan into action. The seeds she had planted earlier today would grow tonight into a full-blown nightmare of a tree, the flesh-eating kind you could never outrun in your nightmares. It was all so simple – and such a classic. And it would be true soon. She felt great. Baby hormones made you that way, she imagined. All warm and fuzzy. Cathy was ready to be a mother to Sebastian's children, and he was going to fulfil that dream for her soon.

Cathy had been staking out Hanna's house for the past four hours and she was bored, growing ever more impatient. Was that idiot friend of hers never going to leave? It was well past 11 p.m., and she was beginning to worry that he intended to stay the night. She'd just wait a little longer...

Finally, her patience was rewarded. 11.30 p.m.. Cathy saw the fool kiss Hanna on the cheek at the door, give her a big hug, jump into his car, and drive off. Time for her evil plan to be activated. She nearly felt sorry for Hanna – it was not what anyone would want to hear, what was coming next. But there were always casualties at war, innocent bystanders. Sebastian was Cathy's, not the plaything of some dumb girl who would leave him in the sort of state that Hanna had left him this afternoon. Cathy felt her indignance rising: she was protecting Sebastian. Hanna was not good enough for him. She needed to be dealt with. *Vigilante justice*.

Cathy got out of her car swiftly, and marched to Hanna's front door. She banged on the door loudly, not giving Hanna a chance not to hear it. Cathy could hear hurried footsteps coming towards the door, and then Hanna yanked it open.

'Oh, it's you...' Hanna looked shocked. She also looked shocking. Her hair was messy, her eyes puffy, her face bloated and blotchy. Hanna clearly didn't cry beautifully. It was disgusting. Cathy managed to hold back the look of revulsion on her face, and plastered on a smile instead.

'May I come in? There is something important I need to say.'

'Oh? Umm, sure – come in.' Hanna had no idea why Cathy wanted to see her.

Cathy strode in, looking for a place to sit down, and found the kitchen table. This would do. She turned to Hanna, eyeing her slow approach into the kitchen. Hanna seemed spaced out. She was a mess. *Time to crank up the heat.*

'Umm, would you like some tea?'

'No, thank you. Please sit down.' Cathy was getting ready for her Oscar-worthy performance.

Hanna sat down opposite Cathy, lost in her grief for a moment. Suddenly remembering she had company, she raised her puffy eyes.

'Hanna, you seemed very upset when you left the office today. I had to come and see you myself. I didn't like the way things were left this afternoon. I thought Sebastian had told you, but I was horrified when I discovered that he hadn't!'

'Told me what?' *What was going on*?

'We had agreed to tell you soon.' Cathy tried to look guilty.

'Yes?' Hanna was very confused. *What the hell was going on*?

'I couldn't hold it back fully this afternoon, as I thought Sebastian was about to break the news to you. It's about my baby, our baby…' Cathy let the words hang in the air. But Hanna wasn't getting it.

'Your baby?'

'Our baby. It was quite unexpected. An accident, really. But now that it has happened, it feels so right. Sebastian is over the moon.'

'Sebastian?' Hanna was even more confused.

'Yes – we hadn't been planning a baby, but it just happened.' Cathy stopped to survey the result of her words. Yes, it was working very well! Hanna looked as if she was ready to fall off the chair, she was so shocked. 'He'd probably told you that we were seeing each other before you came along,' Cathy continued, 'but we broke up when he got involved with you. It just didn't work out. I much prefer to work with him than to sleep with him, if you know what I mean.' Cathy paused, looking for further inspiration. She was coming up with such good stuff on the spot. And Hanna's face was priceless. All this was obviously news to her – well, to both of them, after all! And Hanna had visibly flinched when Cathy mentioned sleeping with Sebastian. That was good. Cathy's job was to hit below the belt, whatever it took to make sure Hanna would never speak to Sebastian again. She had to make Hanna so disgusted with him that she'd never question the validity of Cathy's story. It was a terrible gamble, but Cathy felt she was going to win. She had to. Sebastian was the prize – and he was Cathy's.

'And then I discovered I was expecting,' Cathy continued. 'I had planned to go it alone. But then it all got just too much for me, and I had to tell him. And since he's so clever, he probably would have put two and two together and realised that it was his baby anyhow.'

Cathy stopped to refresh her story. Hanna looked so devastated. Time to focus on her again. 'I was concerned for you this afternoon.'

'Concerned for me?' Hanna didn't understand anything. This nightmare was just too much for her to take. Her world had collapsed today, but it seemed that there was no end to it, that there was still further and further torment ahead to be borne.

'Yes, you looked so upset when you left Sebastian's office. I thought...' *Now, look like you feel really guilty...* 'I thought he had told you about the baby and that's why you were so upset. I wanted to come and see you in person, so that I could explain it all to you. I felt so guilty about it all. I'm sure we can all work it out together. I would love to be your friend.'

Hanna was sinking deeper, and it was obvious to Cathy. *Now, how to bring this up a notch, to end the Hanna/Sebastian saga once and for all*?

'Hanna, I'm so sorry that you are so distressed by all this. I spoke with Sebastian after you left and I was horrified to find that he hadn't told you about the baby. We had agreed to do so very soon. I told him that I wanted to come and see you today in person. He said to go right ahead. He didn't think you'd care.'

*Not care? Not CARE*??

*What planet was he living on? Who was this guy*? Hanna had no idea any more. This was just too much for her. Sebastian was just too cold – she didn't understand him at all. How could he? How could he bed Cathy, make her pregnant, and then go out with Hanna? He had never mentioned that he and Cathy had been an item, either. Who was he? He didn't seem to care about anyone but himself. He hadn't seemed too bothered by the fact that Hanna was going back to Finland, and now this? He didn't even bother to tell her about the baby himself. And he thought *she* didn't care?

Well, she didn't – she didn't care to know anything more about him. Or his two-timing manners. Or his cold heart. How could he treat Cathy the way he had? He thought a baby was no big deal, that Hanna wouldn't be bothered?

Cathy was welcome to him. He was not the man she had thought him to be.

Hanna didn't hear anything more Cathy was saying. A loud, high-pitched din had replaced her hearing. She didn't think her overwrought mind could take account of any more pain, but it was happening. The noise in her ears was giving her the worst headache of her life. Her stomach was heaving. She was going to be sick. She had to get Cathy out, fast.

Somehow, she managed to croak, 'I had no idea. But now, I'm very tired. Thank you for coming.' Somehow, she managed to get up and usher Cathy out the front door. And somehow, she crawled into the living room and curled up on the sofa. She made herself as small as possible. Her life had shrunk to nothing. It was all over. Hanna would go back to Finland straight away, she decided. She could no longer stand it, any of it. Ireland had turned into a nightmare and she had to get out. Now.

## Chapter 9

'Hanna? Are you awake?'

'*Mitä?* Oh, yes, give me a minute.'

Hanna opened her eyes, and tried to take in her surroundings. She was confused for a while, before recalling that she was at home with her mum and dad. And that had been *iskä*, Daddy, calling for her. *Iskä*, being so nice to her, waking her up so gently. So very different from when she had been a teenager, and hadn't wanted to get up in the morning. Back then, he had just shouted at her gruffly, and she had typically shouted something nasty back. And now, here he was, treating her so gently, as if she was just a little girl and not a grown woman. The first tears of the day. It was Christmas, the 24th of December. *It should have been our first Christmas together*, she thought.

Hanna had found Finland changed when she got back: nothing seemed to be the same any more. How could an entire country and a way of life feel so utterly alien after only a year and a half away? People looked strange: the colours had been bleached out of them. Everybody had blond or brown hair, and everyone had tanned skin. People seemed to have grown taller and somehow more erect, righteous. Nobody smiled: they went around with serious, frowning faces. Conversations were short, monotonously matter-of-fact, and muttered in low voices. They were so quiet after the noisy Irish. How had she never noticed before that the Finns were such rigid, boring people?

During those awful last hours in Ireland, Hanna had hung on to the belief that she was going home somewhere familiar and safe. But that had not been the case at all. The language sounded ugly to her ears after the singsong voices of the Irish. If the Irish were enjoying themselves – which they mostly were – or if they were annoyed, you knew: they never could hide anything. But the Finns were masters of the poker face. Their bodies barely moved when they interacted, and everyone seemed to stand very far away from each other.

Hanna was missing Ireland badly. She had been so happy there – a freer version of herself, it had seemed, as if there was something in the air that allowed people to be individuals. Hanna's life had been sweet, even before *he* had entered it. And well before he had ended it. It was all unthinkable now, and Hanna tried her very best to block out the thoughts and images of her previous incarnation.

She felt so lonely. Nobody came close enough to her for her to feel that she was communicating with real humans. Nobody used her name when they spoke to her. She felt that her identity had disappeared. She had become just part of the masses, only as important as the next person as long as she fulfilled her role in the great machine of Finnish society.

Since her arrival, she had spent most of her nights alone in her apartment, watching telly or browsing the internet. Her top-floor, one-bed apartment was in a lovely 1950s part of town, only a few minutes' tram or bus journey outside the city. She had always enjoyed living in her beautiful apartment, which she had decorated with antique furniture and a giant comfy couch, but now it gave her no satisfaction.

The housing estate on which she lived was one of the first purpose-built apartment block areas in the Helsinki suburbs, and had been constructed with a "forest city" philosophy in mind. Thousands of people lived there, yet one could hardly see any of the apartment blocks behind the trees. Hanna had always loved the forests surrounding her building, and before her move to Ireland had been in the habit of going for an evening walk every night on one of the numerous paths through the woods – but even this pleasure had disappeared. Hanna could not face anything beautiful. Going out had become such a hazardous activity: her ever-present tears could spill over at any moment.

Hanna had been politely welcomed back to her job in the concert hall, and everyone had asked how she had got on in Ireland. Her non-committal answers about the beautiful scenery and the nice people had soon made even her most enthusiastic colleagues leave her alone, which was just fine with her.

She mentioned Sebastian to no-one. Those she had already told about him prior to her return learned very quickly not to bring up his name in conversation, after she had informed them that he was a two-timing bastard. Like the fool she had been, she had thought he had loved her, thought that their relationship was so much more than it had been. Now she wanted to neither see him ever again, nor know anything about him. Yet she was plagued by unanswered questions, and haunted by the images of him that constantly invaded her mind.

Her parents had been very understanding and quiet with her, trying to give her space to work things out by herself ever since she had got back. They knew Hanna was miserable, that she had been hurt by a man in Ireland, but they had not demanded to hear the details. Hanna could see that they were concerned, but it was not a Finnish thing to butt into other people's lives uninvited. They did their best to look after her.

Everything was always done for her when she visited her parents, and so it was yet again now, since she had arrived for the Christmas holidays two days previously. All her favourite dinners had been prepared and served up to her, although she didn't have much of an appetite. Hanna had dutifully eaten up every morsel, while her *äiti* kept watch anxiously. Very little had been said about anything at all, and for once, she found herself grateful for the silence. Although she could feel the tension of the unspoken building up, Hanna was used to discomfort by now; she had been back in Finland for almost three months, and her sad little life had settled into a quietly lonely routine.

Micheál had tried to get in touch with Hanna many times during her first month back, but she had ignored all his calls, and had eventually emailed him to say that she'd rather be alone for some time and would contact him when she was ready. He had tried everything – phone calls, texts, emails, Facebook – for a few more weeks, but eventually he had given up. Sofia had got the message a lot quicker, and within a week there wasn't a single peep from her. Anyone else she had got to know in Ireland who had tried to get in touch lost interest quickly when she didn't respond to any of their messages.

Ireland was lost for her, and the quicker Hanna could forget about the place the better. She just needed to continue her little routines day in, day out, and eventually everything would be okay, she kept telling herself, desperately wanting to believe it.

Christmas, *joulu*. The happiest time of the year, or so it had been when she was little. Hanna knew it was going to be a tough day to get through with all the remembered happiness surrounding her. Her little sister Miia, who was now a big girl, a happily-married woman with a baby girl of ten months, Suvi, was coming over today to celebrate Christmas. Hanna was planning to spend as much time as possible with Suvi. She had discovered that for some reason, she was able to forget about her sadness for a while when playing with the adorable little blonde baby, gazing into her huge dark blue eyes. It was as if Hanna could tune into the tiny girl's simple wonderment at her surroundings, her sudden delight in some item that took her fancy. Here was one human being who didn't look at her with guarded pity and concern. Suvi took her as she was, broken heart or no broken heart, as long as the dinner was spooned into her fast enough or her playtime lasted as long as she wanted.

With a heavy sigh, Hanna resolutely made her way to the kitchen, where her *äiti* had Christmas *riisipuuro* – rice porridge – ready for her breakfast, and warm, sweet Christmas fruit "soup" to go with it. She had been reading the newspaper at the kitchen table, but when she heard Hanna enter the room, she sprang into action and spooned a big blob of porridge onto Hanna's plate, sprinkling it with sugar and cinnamon before pouring the fruit soup over it. Not a word had been exchanged, and Hanna was yet again grateful for it. She was concentrating hard on holding back her tears.

Hanna sat down at the kitchen table, and her mother handed over a portion of the newspaper for her to read, just as she always did. Like the rest of the Finns, Hanna had grown up reading her local daily paper, 'Turun Sanomat', while having her breakfast. The familiar routine of reading in silence with her *äiti* was comforting, and as she slowly ate the delicious Christmas breakfast, she began to feel gradually more composed and at peace.

Hanna's sister Miia's family bustled in around 11 a.m., and Hanna made a beeline for her niece. Suvi was on fine form, and giggled delightedly when she saw Hanna. Hanna smiled back, and it felt like a true smile, not the forced imitations she had been flashing at the people around her for months now. *Thank God one doesn't have to smile a lot in Finland, or I would have no hope of survival*, she thought.

At noon, the family gathered around the telly to listen to the announcement of Christmas peace, declared every Christmas continuously since the late Middle Ages from the old capital of Finland, Turku. Hanna and her family had gone to listen to it on numerous occasions while she was growing up there. Hanna could remember the crowds that had always gathered well in advance, stamping their feet on the white ground to keep warm in the freezing weather, with breath-smoke rising all around, while the marching band played traditional songs. The wait had always been agonisingly long and boring when she had been a child. But now she found herself comforted by the familiar Christmas ceremonies, and vowed to forget about her troubles for at least that one day.

After an hour or two of playing with the happy toddler, it was Hanna's turn to go to the *joulusauna* to freshen up for the main event. Sauna, the only Finnish word (apart from Nokia) to have entered into international language, was the epicentre of Christmas celebrations, and the only properly hot building in the extreme Finnish winter. A Finn could not sit down for his or her

Christmas meal without a thorough sauna session first. Hanna lay down on the upper level of her parents' sauna seats, and aimed a throw of water onto the stones of the *kiuas* – Sauna stove. It was an art form to manipulate the big timber spoon from her awkward prone position. The water splashed onto the stove with a mighty roar. The hot steam reached her a few seconds later, and she groaned with pleasure. After only a few minutes she was dripping with sweat. The familiar routine worked magic on her frayed nerves, and she found herself beginning to relax.

*There are very few things more pleasurable than the few minutes of sitting down outside on the terrace to cool down in between sauna visits*, Hanna thought, as she emerged from the cool shower after her sauna, wrapping herself up in her bathrobe. In the past, she had enjoyed the tradition of drinking "sauna–beer" as much as the next Finn, but found now that she did not miss it.

*I know I have everything I need.* Tears yet again sprang to her eyes, but this time she let them come, let them slowly drip down her already-wet face. As she cried noiselessly, the ever-present heaviness began gradually to lift; as she said that sentence to herself over and over again, she could feel her ribcage opening up.

*He* had forever repeated that sentence to her, and had spent hours on end explaining its meaning to her. The theory of the universe, the higher self and the connection to it had all been part of his everyday jargon. She had loved to snuggle up to him on the sofa, listening to his hypnotic words. Her heart was breaking all over again, as the memories came flooding back to her. She let them come.

Hanna still couldn't believe what Sebastian had done, messing around with Cathy, who was carrying his child, and at the same time being so convincingly "in love" with her. Part of her difficulty in believing was that it all felt so out of character for the Sebastian she had grown to know and to love – not at all like the kind and wonderful person she had thought him to be. Perhaps his never having actually said he loved her was an attempt at honesty: if he didn't say the words, it didn't count. But his actions had implied it all, and Hanna had thought he cared a lot more than he obviously had.

She had always thought of herself as a good judge of character, but she had been completely wrong about him. She didn't trust anyone any more; anyone could be just as two-faced as Sebastian had been, and she now knew she was not capable of recognising the difference between true and false. She had loved Sebastian deeply – still loved him – and it had all been meaningless to him. Well – at least she had spent three of the most wonderful months anyone could ask for with him, and if that was all she could have in her lifetime, then so be it.

Despite his having played her so cruelly, Hanna still believed that his positive-thinking teachings were correct, that there was truth behind the concepts and ideas he had explained to her. She would have to learn to make her peace with her decision to leave Sebastian. She knew in her heart that she would not have been able to accept and to live with the impossible love-triangle that had been going on behind her back. *I have everything I need to create more:* she had to learn to believe it, that her time with him had been just a small step along her life path, and that there was something more for her in the future. She would work to change the meaning of their short relationship, to learn to regard it as a brief, wonderful holiday, in order for her to be able to continue her life.

Today Hanna began to feel that she might after all possess the inner strength to find new meaning in her seemingly barren life. She started to see a way that she could survive. The Finns thought that the sauna had magical qualities, and today Hanna joined their ranks. She felt cleansed inside and out. As yet, her hope was only the merest green shoot, breaking the surface of the earth for the first time, yet it was real.

Christmas dinner, as always, was a mighty feast. Her *äiti* always prepared it so carefully. The gigantic ham had been roasted in the oven overnight at a low temperature, her mother getting up several times specially to check on its progress. The whole family sat down at the table, full of cheerful chatter, with Suvi holding court noisily in her baby seat at the end. She flashed toothy grins in all directions, fresh from a long, late-afternoon nap after many hours of play with Hanna.

'Help yourselves, everyone,' Hanna's *äiti* announced and Hanna discovered she was ravenous. It seemed that her appetite had also decided to join the land of the living. She smiled to herself, and jumped up from her seat to join the queue that had formed in front of the cooker, where her mother had placed the *joululaatikot* – Christmas casseroles. 'Leave some for me,' Hanna exclaimed, as her brother-in-law Jukka piled carrot, turnip, potato and liver casseroles on his plate as if they were going out of fashion. Jukka had a notoriously huge appetite, and Hanna had always watched with fascination as mountains of food disappeared inside him, leaving not a trace of the man's enormous appetite on his muscular torso. He was a big man, two metres tall; his blond hair had started to recede upwards around the temples and forehead, but it didn't seem to lessen his good looks. Hanna had noticed her sister throwing appreciative glances in his direction all day. Miia looked like she'd be in the mood for trying for another little Suvi tonight.

'I've missed this ham!' Hanna found herself exclaiming at the table, where she had devoured the big slice her father had cut from the roasted pig. There was nothing that tasted quite like her *äiti's* Christmas ham. And it went so well with the *rosolli*, a salad of diced carrots, onion, pickled gherkins and apple. Suvi was also enjoying it all noisily, as Miia spooned the casseroles into her mouth, followed with a few pieces of diced carrot.

*I would have liked to have children one day*, Hanna found herself thinking, gazing at Suvi. She was just such a lovely little girl. Hanna resolved to spend more time with her niece since there was no chance now for her own unborn children to come to Planet Earth. *He will be the father of Cathy's child soon*, she thought, frowning at the pain. The child was due in about three months. *It should have been mine*.

She had secretly started to entertain daydreams about a family with Sebastian during those golden months with him, but that would never happen now. A small part of her regretted that she hadn't accidentally got pregnant before she came back to Finland. At least then she would have had some part of him with her always, even though the man himself was lost to her. He was a bastard – that much was clear – but Hanna could not stop yearning for him. It was like a disease that was eating away at her. Feeling her appetite suddenly falter, she got up from the table, excusing herself.

As she reached the bathroom, she sat down on the loo seat and put her head in her hands. It was all so difficult. Would she ever get over this? After a while, she heard a gentle tap at the door – her *äiti*, wondering if Hanna was ready to come out. 'In a minute,' she called to her mother. She looked at herself in the mirror. Not too bad. Only a few tears had managed to escape at the corners of her eyes, and she looked pretty normal.When she returned to the kitchen, everyone was quiet except Suvi, who was keeping up her own noisy entertainment.

Hanna's mother cleared up the empty dinner plates and invited everyone to come and take some dessert. It was, as always, rice porridge, the same as her breakfast had been. As they took their plates of porridge, her family joked with each other about the piece of almond hidden in it. The person that found it would have good luck for the year and could make a wish, but nobody was supposed to dig for it while serving themselves. Eventually, the coveted nut surfaced in Hanna's portion, rousing an over-the-top cheer from the rest of her family. They knew she was very unhappy, but there seemed to be so little they could do about it.

After they left the table, Hanna's father gave her arm a quick squeeze and a smile – an unusual demonstration of affection from him, and one which made Hanna feel a bit better. She could feel her family willing her to keep going, not to give up hope – or at the very least to behave herself through the Christmas evening – and she felt comforted.

Hanna lifted Suvi out of her chair, to the little girl's utter delight. She always seemed to be happiest when she was moving, as if a stationary life was not one worth living. This time, their trip took them to the living room, where they sat in their usual seats to wait for Santa to arrive with the presents. Only Jukka was missing, gone to take out the rubbish. Hanna bounced Suvi up and down on the floor, the little girl squealing with delight at each bounce. After a minute or two, the doorbell rang and Miia ran out to open it, looking happy and flushed. It was Santa, and he marched into the living room with the usual '*onkos täällä kilttejä lapsia*?', or 'are there any good children around here?'

Suvi's mouth hung open. She had never seen anything like it yet during her ten months of life. Luckily, she was not scared – just surprised to see the enormous white-bearded man in red, a strange man who had a present for Suvi as well as everyone else. Hanna found herself laughing alongside the rest of the family, including Santa. She laughed so much that she had tears in her eyes again – the best kind. Santa asked Miia to sing a Christmas song for him, which she did, blushing prettily, and then he left. Jukka, coming in from successfully disposing of the rubbish, couldn't believe he had missed Santa again!

That evening, when Hanna had retired to bed, her *äiti* knocked on the door and came in. She sat at the end of Hanna's bed, just the way she used to when Hanna was little. She asked Hanna how she was feeling now. Hanna murmured that she was okay.

'I understand it can be hard to adjust to being back after being away for so long, but it has been three months now,'

Hanna's mother said, looking at Hanna directly. 'What happened to you in Ireland that has you so upset? Was it that man you met over there?'

'Yes.'

It felt good to Hanna to be able to admit it.

'I thought so. Normally these things will find a way to sort themselves out, if you just let them. Life is a bit hard at times, but all the same, it goes on. I was engaged once, when I was very young, but my fiancé died in a car accident. It was hard – but I got over it. I found your dad. And we had you two girls.'

This was new information to Hanna, and she stared at her mother's profile. *Äiti* had always been a stern and quiet figure, and she looked sad now as she sat there, at the end of Hanna's bed, lost in thought. Hanna had never known that her mother had suffered in love. Her *äiti* didn't talk about her past much. Anything Hanna knew about it, she had had to worm out of her mother by asking endless questions over the years. Sometimes her mother would disclose a fragment of something, but very often she did not, simply saying that she couldn't remember.

Tonight, though, *äiti* had opened up a little, and somehow her mother's revelation was the most comforting thing Hanna had heard during the past months' nightmare. It was obvious that it had taken a lot for her mother to tell her about her past heartache.

After a while her mother got up, said goodnight and left the room. Hanna closed her eyes, falling asleep quickly. She slept peacefully, without any dreams.

*

'Hanna? We are going to have a sauna evening on Friday night, will you come?'

'I don't think I can. I promised to go to Turku to help out my sister with the baby this weekend.' The lie slipped out so quickly. Hanna had become very efficient at inventing excuses for not attending any kind of social events. Back in Helsinki, it was still just her and her apartment every evening, and even the thought of breaking the routine made Hanna's head spin. She was out of practice at doing anything outside the precious routine that shielded her from the world. She got up every morning and went to work. She tuned pianos all day long, hardly playing for pleasure any more. She went home, watched telly or messed about on the Internet, and went to bed. She had tried to resume her walks in the forests surrounding her building, but all that beauty still got to her, tugging at her heartstrings. It was safer not to go anywhere, just in case.

Since Christmas, Hanna had developed a keen interest in watching competitive sports of all kinds on the TV. She couldn't really watch any kind of romantic programmes: sex was completely banned on her watch list, and even kissing was a step too far – she just couldn't take it. Ice hockey, on the other hand, was just brilliant, and she had discovered a growing passion for TPS, a team from her home town of Turku – even though she had lived in the capital, Helsinki, for a long time. Luckily for her, TPS was doing well this season. Just the right kind of therapy for getting over a broken heart: bulky men covered in protective gear from head to toe – Hanna found this therapeutically symbolic – fighting over a stupid little *kiekko* – puck. Frivolous yet not-girly-emotional activity was exactly what she needed. She couldn't take anything that might remind her that she was a woman, with a woman's heart and needs. Gender thinking was on her banned list. She had even contemplated cutting her hair short, but as this would involve going to a hairdresser, and possibly even having to make some sort of small talk, the idea had been quickly scrapped.

Hanna's self-developed therapy of emotionally-cleansing-yet-not-personally-involved sport spectating seemed to be working. Nowadays, she found herself wanting to burst into tears for no apparent reason only once a day on average, a massive improvement on her pre-Christmas state. She found herself thinking often about her mother's revelation of her dead fiancé. She could so easily relate to that story. The Sebastian she had fallen in love with was dead also – not killed, but as good as, as far as she was concerned. Sometimes Hanna couldn't stop the feelings of utter betrayal from invading her mind and body. She had fallen twice, so heavily. First, in love. Then into this black place of despair where she could barely hang on to life.

But her mother had got over a man – and so would she, at whatever cost. She would put on a stern Finnish face, square her shoulders and with pure *sisu* – that mythical force of inner strength that only Finns possessed – she would get through this torment.

## *Chapter 10*

Pyhätunturi ski resort: one meter of snow, minus two degrees Celsius, and glorious, skin-burning sunshine until ten o'clock in the evening. What could be better than that?

Hanna couldn't believe how quickly she had been able to turn her life around, once she had made the decision to do it. Having felt so miserable for so long, she had barely recognised the feelings associated with happiness. *But it is all in the head*, Hanna mused, *just like* he *always said*. She had decided to make herself better, to continue her life. Sebastian had taught her about the scale of emotions, from depression to joy, through anger, finding new perspectives and hopefulness. She recognised that she had completed all the steps on the emotional scale: she had spent a lot of time in depression and anger, raging one minute and weeping at the hopelessness of it all the next. Eventually, Hanna discovered that putting the matter into a wider context took her on a step above anger and hurt – and her mother's story of her lost love had fulfilled this admirably.

She needed a holiday, she had decided. On her own, somewhere where nobody knew her, as she was still not ready to face her usual social circle. And an active holiday, too: it was time to leave the ice-hockey season alone and actually go out to *do* something herself, for a change. Since it was April, and the best skiing season was in full swing in Lapland, she would get herself onto a night train, pack her skis and get on the slopes.

'This is the first day of my new life!' Hanna had shouted out loud to herself, in front of her mirror. It was so corny that it managed to draw a smile out of her. Sebastian had always told her this, but now she truly believed him. Hopeful for her new life, Hanna could feel the butterflies of excitement in her lower stomach. She had forgotten how *that* felt, too!

She had enjoyed her stay on the overnight train that had taken her from Helsinki to Kemijärvi. She slept well, soothed by the continuous movement of the train, and a sense of adventure that she hadn't felt for far too long. Being out of her apartment at last felt amazing – freedom from her self-imposed prison. Hanna could only feel awe at the power of acceptance: it was powerful stuff.

Hanna had family everywhere in Lapland, probably even in the ski resort in which she was staying. Hanna's parents' home wasn't too far by Lapland standards, but she had never been to Pyhätunturi (the "Holy Mountain") before. *Since excitement is the organising principle in life, let it do its magic here now*, Hanna had thought, dumping her gear at the concierge desk of her hotel. Straight away a good-looking young man came to the rescue, guiding her to the reception desk to check in, while promising to guard her gear. And he had smiled. *A smiling Finn! Miracles don't cease to happen!* Hanna had thought.

It had been a few years since Hanna had last been on a ski slope, and as she stood at the top of the lowest piste, she remembered with a sickening lurch that she was actually terrified of downhill skiing. *Well, too late now*, she said to herself resolutely. *Here's to my new, exciting life!* There was no turning back. Taking a deep breath and fighting down her fear, she pushed off. The speed was exhilarating. Hanna's delight surged upwards within her. If this was an omen for her new life, it was a good one. She headed towards the ski lift to find another good omen to last a lifetime.

Hanna was on the piste for hours without noticing the time. It was only when her tummy began making ravenous noises that she was able to drag herself away from the slopes, spent but filled with joy. There was something very therapeutic about a physical activity that gave you a near death-experience, she decided, smiling. And now, *ruokaa* – food!

Hanna enjoyed her dinner. Her reindeer stew was delicious, very similar to the one her granny had used to make. So hungry was she that she ordered a starter and a main course, and was even contemplating a dessert – ice cream with *hilla* (cloudberry). She had endured countless painful afternoons picking the small orange berries throughout her childhood summers. It was no mean feat: they only grew in the boglands of the north, which were also inhabited by the terror of Lapland's summer skies, mosquitoes. The little buggers loved to bite humans – a great change to their usual diet of reindeer and brown bears. As it took a week of torment before she became immune to them, Hanna remembered always spending the first week of her summer holidays scratching and scratching – and then scratching some more. Her greatest joy had been spending a bit of time each evening before bedtime getting her revenge, as her *kärpäslätkä* – fly swat – busily tracked and killed hordes of mosquitoes. Her mother had not been too impressed by the blobs of blood all over their campervan walls – invariably the insects seemed to have taken a bite out of somebody before meeting their end.

Giving no further thought to her childhood summer torturers, she enjoyed every morsel of her delicious dessert. The waiter approached her to collect her empty glass bowl.

'Did you enjoy that?'

'Yes, thank you, absolutely delightful!' Hanna was in a good mood. It felt great to be smiling again.

'Are you going to the dance later on in the ballroom?' the waiter asked. 'We have a great band playing tonight.'

A dance! Hanna hadn't been to a ballroom dance for a long time. As a keen lover of music and dancing, during her teens she had briefly considered making a career in dancing, so much had she loved it. She had begun attending the still-prevalent traditional dances when she was 14 – her rock-and-roll dance partner had dragged her down to one, and taught her how to dance the popular versions of the ballroom classics. She loved the foxtrot and the waltz. Her particular favourite was the Finnish fast polka – ow, there was a dance to get you out of breath!

Hanna thought there was something wondrous about dancing together with another person, creating matching movements with their own momentum. She had been disappointed to learn that the ballroom tradition had mostly died out in Dublin. Traditional Irish dancing, though, was still alive and well, and she had attended classes in set dancing, and even learnt some basics of solo dancing – the Riverdance style.

But to attend a dance tonight… Hanna felt excitement stirring inside her. She had been in her sorrowful hibernation for so long – that's what the land of eternal winter, Hibernia, had done to her. Would she go? Yes, she would.

Hanna's heart was beating rapidly when she entered the ballroom. The dancehall band was playing a slow set of foxtrots. The music was heart-wrenchingly melancholic, just the way it should be, and Hanna felt better. For the first time since her return, Hanna felt a proper connection to Finnish culture. She could at last say it was good to be home.

The song finished, and Hanna hurried across the dancefloor to line up along the wall with the other girls. The men hovered some distance from the ladies, eyeing them up. In the early days of her dancehall attendance, Hanna had quickly learned to push her way to stand at the front of the often three or four deep line of women, in order to get picked – she had no interest in sitting down to watch other people dancing when she could be up there enjoying herself.

Having found a prime position, Hanna straight away received a bow and a stretched-out arm from a good-looking young man in lieu of a verbal offer. Hanna accepted his hand, feeling eager, as she realised how much she had missed dancing. The pair heard the opening rhythms of a fast, cheerful foxtrot and lined up quickly. Off they went, moving to the fast beat skilfully and with long strides. Hanna sighed with pleasure: her partner was well practised in leading, and she closed her eyes to fully enjoy the purposeful movement of two bodies to the rhythm.

The first dance finished, but it was customary to dance two dances with the same partner, as the band always played two songs of the same style and tempo. Hanna waited beside her partner for the second dance to start, smiling happily. He asked her about how she was enjoying her holiday, and she answered briefly but courteously – she was enjoying it well, thank you. She wasn't looking for discussion, and her polite but firmly discouraging body language made this clear. Her dance partner got the message, and smiled at Hanna humorously. From his dialect Hanna could tell that he was also from the south, probably from around Helsinki.

The band struck up the second dance, and they began to move again. It felt good to be held by another human being again after so long. It was such a safe way to enjoy bodily contact, without having to actually give the other person any real attention. Hanna noted that her partner's body was well-toned; he was the perfect height for her, and his lead was firm and fluid. *An ideal dance partner – and also ideally quiet.*

The song drew to an end too soon, and Hanna offered her hand so that he could escort her back to the ladies' line. As he bowed to her to acknowledge her return, he asked if he could request a dance again later that night. Hanna quickly agreed. He had been an excellent partner, so why not?

Two hours later, the band announced that the next hour was going to be ladies' choice. Hanna hadn't yet missed a single dance, and she was feeling great. Skiing and dancing in the same day – bliss! She was starting to feel the physical effects of so much strenuous exercise in one day, but she didn't care. If she couldn't get out of bed the next day, she would just stay in it.

Hanna lined up and found herself opposite her first dance partner of the evening. Despite his request, he had not yet asked her to dance with him again – but he was now grinning at her in such a fashion that she could not resist. She put out her hand to him – he took it quickly, and led her onto the floor.

'My name is Jarno – what is yours?'

Hanna thought about this for a few seconds, but since she was having so much fun, she didn't think there was any harm in telling him. He smiled, and led her into a blissful slow waltz, again showing his expert skill in this dance so often regarded as difficult. Hanna was in heaven.

After their first dance, Jarno turned to Hanna.

'Could I be so bold as to suggest that we dance a few more sets after this? You are the best dancer here tonight.'

'Okay.' This came out so fast that Hanna didn't havc time to stop it. But sure, what harm could there be in more time with this fabulous dancer? He seemed to understand her not wanting to talk, and as it was ladies' hour, it suited her fine. Finnish men were often very eager on the dance floor, and so could sometimes get the wrong impression, starting to suggest extracurricular activities all too quickly, particularly when they had a few drinks in them. For now, Hanna was happy to be led by this nicely-shaped body, the owner of which understood the need to keep his mouth shut.

The evening flew by, and Hanna found herself dancing the rest of it with Jarno, who had demonstrated his skill in every type of dance the band had managed to throw at them. Hanna was feeling very hot – not only from the physical exertion, to her great surprise. She had found her body responding to Jarno's as they moved together – and that was a feeling she had not experienced for a long time.

The last waltz was over. Jarno was still holding her hand. Hanna made up her mind and pulled Jarno towards the doors, up the stairs and into her room. She had not finished her day of exercise yet.

*

Hanna slowly gained consciousness. The first thing she noticed was that she felt satisfied. The second was that she was sore all over. She opened her eyes and sighed in relief when she noticed that the other side of her bed was empty. She had not been looking forward to facing Jarno this morning, and he had obviously read her mind and decided to go. He had been an excellent lover. Just as he had been skilled and passionate on the dance floor, with great stamina, so had he been in bed. And the best part was that he had kept his mouth shut, apart from his groans of pleasure. Small talk had not been on her agenda.

Hanna rolled over. As she stretched luxuriously, she noticed a business card on the side table. Jarno, it turned out, was a personal trainer – no wonder he hadn't run out of steam. As she had suspected, he was based in Helsinki, and not far from the National Concert Hall. On the back of the card, he had written "thank you" – and added an invitation to phone him if she wanted to repeat their night of "Dance & Passion".

Unable to face the slopes that day, after an indulgent room-service breakfast and a couple more hours of sleep, Hanna opted for the spa experience her hotel had to offer. She wrapped herself in the sumptuous bathrobe hanging on her bathroom door and flip-flopped her way to the spa. A quick, screamy dip in the outdoor cold pool had her running for the sauna, where a firm-faced Finnish matron was throwing water on the rocks of the *kiuas*. The stinging steam hit Hanna and she covered her face with her hands, in order to breathe until the steam disappeared, leaving an enjoyable tingle on her skin. *Time for a dip in the cold pool, and then into that beautifully warm jacuzzi*, thought Hanna.

*Miracles list.*

The thought popped into Hanna's head. Perhaps it was time to start counting her blessings so that she could heal, and move on in her life. This whole trip was all about that anyway – it was high time to start practising. What miracles could she find in her life?

*Her parents, her sister and her niece.*

Well, that was an easy start. Hanna genuinely felt that she was blessed to have the family she did. Her heart started to glow, just a little.

*Finland.*

She did truly love her home country. Taught from an early age that it was like winning the lotto to be born in Finland, she could appreciate its untouched nature and the calmness of the people. Admittedly, it was always going to be hard to find a bad word to say about any country while lying down in a whirlpool of warm water, looking up at the sky through a glass ceiling, hoping that even the northern lights would appear to brighten her day.

*My work.*

Piano tuning was such an exciting skill. Even after all these years, Hanna found that no two pianos were the same. She would always have to assess the personality of an instrument before she began work. There was nothing mechanical about working on an entity with a soul of its own, expressed through the symbiosis of player and instrument. Hanna decided to begin playing again, to let music flow through her and heal her. She had avoided playing the piano in any serious way since her arrival back to Finland, but now she began to feel she could face it again.

*Well, listing out your miracles does actually work*, Hanna thought, as she felt her body relaxing in the water.

And perhaps she *would* meet up with Mr "Dance & Passion" when she got back to Helsinki.

## *Chapter 11*

Sebastian woke with a start. He was covered in sweat and his heart was pounding. It was dark in the room. He had been dreaming a dream so real, and he was still inside it, moving it along in his mind even though he knew he had woken up. Hanna had been there: he had been running, looking for her, but had not found her, even though he knew she was somewhere near. Sebastian had been panicking, running from room to room in a house that was his but wasn't, the way locations never make sense in dreams, looking for Hanna. Even in the dream he had known that she was gone, unattainable.

Sebastian found his heartbeat slowing down. Sighing heavily, he put the light on and got up to go to the bathroom. Only now he took in his surroundings: he was in a suite on the legendary 'Queen Mary' Atlantic cruise liner, now a hotel and a tourist attraction in Long Beach. When Cathy had informed him that she had managed to swing a gig for him at a personal development conference in Los Angeles, he had known straight away where he wanted to stay. The Queen Mary was the ultimate English art deco masterpiece. Why the Brits had let it go to Long Beach was a total mystery to him. None of the other liners from the golden era of Atlantic travel had survived. The Americans were very proud of the Queen Mary, as it had played a crucial role in World War II as a troops carrier. It was the love of art deco that inspired Sebastian, but now he found himself not being able to enjoy it. It all felt meaningless.

Sebastian washed his face and went to look at the time. 4.30 a.m. By now he knew from experience that when he had a Hanna nightmare, there was no chance of him getting back to sleep. He put on some casual clothes and sat down at the armchair by the dark window, resigning himself to the usual mental pain. No amount of learning to maintain his calm could help him; he had found that his strong belief in being the master creator of his own life had been severely affected.

*Hanna.*

Why had she left the way she did? It was four months now since she had gone back to Finland, and there had been no word from her. Not that he had been expecting it, the way she had left, but he couldn't help hoping that she'd change her mind and come back, or at least contact him. He had tormented himself trying to understand why she had suddenly turned completely against him, refusing to see him during the last day of her stay in Ireland, telling him in no uncertain terms that she never wanted to see or hear from him again. 'Please do not contact me,' she had said during the last horrible phone call they had shared. Her voice had been dripping with rage.

Why? Why was she furious? He had been more than willing to give a long-distance relationship a try. Hell, he had even been willing to move over to Finland and to commute from there, but he had never been given a chance to voice this. One day, Hanna had just told him to get lost. She had vanished from his life as if she had never been there.

He didn't have her Finnish phone number, and her Irish phone had been disconnected as soon as she was gone. Her email address had been cancelled, she had removed him from her Facebook friends list, and he never had got her address in Finland, as there was never any need to know it when she lived in Ireland. He had tried to Google her, but only a mention of her having a job in the Helsinki concert hall had come up – no contact details. He phoned the Helsinki concert hall asking for her phone number, but the chilly lady at the other end had refused to give it to him.

Sebastian tried to locate Hanna's friend Micheál, but as he couldn't even remember his last name, the task had been futile. How could a person vanish from the face of the earth like this? The only thing he could do, but had not yet tried, was to fly to Finland and hope to confront her outside the Helsinki concert hall. But this seemed so brutal somehow, especially after she had told him not to contact her ever again. He couldn't face seeing Hanna's beautiful face distorted with anger towards him. It would break his heart all over again.

Back in Ireland, by contrast, Sofia had given Hanna hardly any thought. When Micheál had demanded that she meet up with him so that he could continue agonising over Hanna's actions, Sofia hadn't seen any need for it. As far as she was concerned, that was Hanna's business, and her business only, and Sofia certainly wasn't going to butt in where she was not wanted. Hanna had got that message across very clearly, when Sofia had tried to contact her just after she returned home. Sofia agreed with Micheál that it was a pity Hanna had changed her mind about Sebastian. Sofia could have sworn that it had been the real deal, so severe had been the symptoms. But then one day, Hanna had just packed her bags and gone back to Finland, without a word to anybody – so it mustn't have been real, after all.

Sofia was never going back to Finland, that much she knew for sure. She loved her life in Ireland, and thought of her soft adopted country with great fondness. Hanna had made her read *Gone With the Wind* and its sequel, *Scarlett*, and Sofia had adored a particular scene in the sequel. The all-American Scarlett, visiting Ireland, learned that a "soft" day was one on which it rained, but gently, refreshingly.

Sofia was a firm believer that nationalities are formed and influenced heavily by their climate. Finland's weather patterns were incredibly extreme, from 30 degrees of nightless summer to minus 30 degrees of dayless winter – and everything in between. When it rained, it poured – in the summer, with thunder storms, and in the winter, with snow storms. The people were the same: extremists in many ways, hot and cold, calm and crazy. There were no homeless people in Finland – firstly, because they would die in the winter, and secondly, because the society was far too practical: nobody wanted to be looking at them and their misery. Misery must be hidden away behind closed doors at all cost. Practical.

The Irish, on the other hand, were soft like the refreshing rain: no extremes, no strong social consciousness, no great tragedies, apart from the old hurt caused by the English. The Irish let their hearts rule their heads most of the time. And yet homeless people were allowed to be on the streets. People gave them money, but nobody really did anything about it at the national level. Perhaps, thought Sofia, they even revelled a little in the visible manifestations of misery on their own doorsteps. One needed to be reminded about how lucky one really was in life, and that one could help a little. Softly, softly, like the rain. It could not really create any real havoc, nor could it really nourish the soil enough. Harmless. Yet Sofia knew which type of rain she preferred.

*Ah, the deepness of my thoughts*, Sofia mused. Lately, she had been able to see everything so clearly. She was permanently in a good mood nowadays. Aaron, her Aussie, had stayed on to work and he was just brilliant, so good with her horses. There was never really any rain in his part of Australia. No wonder he brought such sunshine.

Micheál, meanwhile, had been devastated by Hanna's disappearance. He spent countless nights at home, unable to muster the get-up-and-go attitude required to resume his hectic schedule on the Dublin scene. Hanna had abandoned him, without a word. He was so miserable that he only had energy for his couch and the telly. He couldn't understand why his favourite girl didn't want to stay in touch with him, and it hurt. He had always been afraid that someday some gorgeous hunk of a guy would come and break his heart – but this pining after a woman had left him speechless. He certainly had not seen it coming.

Micheál had tried to ring Sofia a few times to discuss Hanna's strange disappearance, but Sofia didn't seem to think there was anything odd about it. Sofia insisted on describing Hanna's silence as "just a Finnish thing", and Micheál felt helpless.

How could another culture be that different? How could Hanna first be the best of friends with him, and then one day, turn around and just say, "So long"? That was cold, even for the cold Finns. But then again, how well did he really know the girl? Maybe Hanna had only considered him a sort of holiday fling, someone convenient to spend time with while abroad before going back to her real life.

From Sofia, Micheál had sensed certain arrogance about the Finns – but Hanna was not like that – how could she be? That would mean that she hadn't felt the same way about him, and that thought wounded him too deeply. With the amount of pain swirling around inside him, it seemed incredible that more could be found – and yet it seemed to have endless powers of self-perpetuation.

Micheál was only half-concentrating at work, and found that he was not as passionate about organising parties and soireés as he had been. Soon he would risk losing clients, as he couldn't keep on faking happiness forever. What was it all for? There had been something special about Hanna. Micheál felt that she had understood him at a level that nobody else had ever done – she had got him perfectly and accepted him just as he was. There hadn't really been a day when they had not been in touch, even during the headiest early days of the Sebastian romance, and she had trusted him with everything. Until the last days of her stay in Ireland, and ever since her arrival back in her native country.

*It's hard to believe that we had only been friends for just over a year*, Micheál thought. It had been full-on, and he had felt a connection with her that was timeless. Hanna had filled a gap he hadn't known he had in his life – until it was too late.

*I can't let her go.*

Micheál decided that he would find a way to bring Hanna back into his life, whatever that took. Although he didn't know Sofia well, he did know that she was involved in natural horsemanship, and he found her address on Google. Therefore, on a summery April afternoon he headed off to drive to Sofia's stables, in order to have a good chat with her about Hanna.

After the inevitable wrong turns, he eventually drove down the wooded lane to Sofia's paradise. The view over Dublin bay from her hilly location was stunning, and Micheál could feel the sunshine heating his deep-chilled bones. He suddenly felt convinced he was going to get Hanna back, and was delighted to be standing in Sofia's delivery yard – apart from the smell of horse manure.

'Micheál! Good to see you. How are things? Have you heard from Hanna? She hasn't been in touch since she left. How is she?'

Micheál's hopes were dashed. He had believed that Sofia would hold the magic key to unlocking Hanna's mystery disappearance, but it seemed that it was not meant to be.

'I was hoping that you'd be able to tell me that. I haven't been able to get in touch with her since she disappeared, and I really hoped that she had been in touch with you. My emails to her aren't getting through, and I don't have a phone number for her.'

'No, she hasn't been in touch. She left a voicemail on my phone when she was leaving the country, but she didn't leave a phone number for Finland. I know that she works at the National Concert Hall, tuning their pianos. Have you tried to ring them?' Sofia asked, wiping the muck off her hands.

'No, I don't know how to find them. Finnish is all gobbledygook to me!'

'Ah, yes, not an easy language. Why don't I Google it now and give you a number to ring?' Sofia began marching towards her house at top speed. It seemed to Micheál that the girl didn't do anything slowly. She had this highly effective and purposeful air about her. Hanna had a touch of it, but she had always seemed much softer.

Sofia plonked herself in front of a laptop and furiously tapped in a few words. While Micheál blinked, she scribbled down some numbers for him to try. Fast was nothing on this girl.

'Here, try these – and take no nonsense from the Finns. When they tell you that they can't give you her phone number or other contact details, just tell them that it is a matter of emergency.' Sofia smiled and got up. The audience was clearly over.

'Thanks a lot!' Micheál managed to say, as he followed Sofia back down to his car. Only when he had been driving for several minutes did he realise that he had not seen any sign of Sofia missing her friend, or any touch of sentimentality. Nor had Sofia offered to contact Finland on his behalf: it seemed that he'd been lucky to get the few scribbled digits from her. *Such strange behaviour*, Micheál thought. Would he ever manage to understand these cold, rash Finns? His own Hanna had seemed so lovely, but had left him just as cruelly as Sofia had just now dismissed him.

He was going to have to make a most-likely-to-be-very-humiliating phone call to Finland tomorrow, to beg yet another cold-blooded Finn to release Hanna's contact details to him. Yet he was willing to go through any amount of embarrassment in order to hear Hanna's voice again.

*

Hanna's phone was ringing. She fished it out of her handbag and looked at the number. Her heart missed a beat. An Irish number.

*Who could it be? Would it be him? How did he find me?* raced through Hanna's mind. Her hands were shaking. She could not answer.

Finally, the phone stopped ringing. Distractedly, Hanna put it down on the piano she had been working on. As a rule, she never put anything on her pianos, as the finish could get marked very easily, and she was horrified when she realised what she had done. She detested people who were sloppy with other people's instruments. The concert pianists were always leaving dirty tissues and pencils in her Concert Hall pianos, and she could have kicked them. She quickly removed the phone, relieved that it had not marked the piano.

Hanna sat in a daze. *Who had tracked her down*? As if in answer, her phone beeped to tell her that she had a message. She picked it up with trembling hands and looked at the screen. *A voice message*. She put it down again.

*Am I strong enough to hear his voice?* It could easily be someone else – but who else would go to the trouble of tracking her down, when she had not given her new number to anyone in Ireland?

*I have to know*, Hanna decided. She picked up her Nokia, and dialled her voicemail.

'Um, this is Micheál here. I'm hoping to reach Hanna Suvanto. I hope I have the right number. Hanna, darling, please, if this is your phone, please, please, please ring me back! I'm missing you so much. I don't understand how you could abandon me so cruelly. So – call me back straight away, don't leave me wondering if I got the right number. Hanna, please, from the bottom of my heart, ring me,' she heard Micheál's voice pleading.

Hanna felt tears spring to her eyes. It felt so awful and yet so good to hear Micheál's voice. Before she could talk herself out of it, she hit the redial button. After a few seconds, she heard the familiar Irish tones. She was finding it hard to breathe.

'Hello? Hanna, is that you?' Micheál's voice called.

'Yes, Micheál, it is me.'

'Oh, Hanna, thank God! What happened? Are you all right? Why didn't you get back to me? How could you disappear like that?' All Micheál's pent-up concern rushed forth.

'I'm okay now – getting better. I just couldn't face anything Irish. I've missed you, though. It is so lovely to hear your voice.'

'You too, dear. But what happened?'

'I'd rather not talk about it. But tell me about you – how are you?' Hanna changed the subject.

'Okay since I tracked you down! It wasn't easy convincing that madam in the Helsinki Concert Hall that she needed to give me your phone number – I nearly had to threaten to kill her.'

Hanna laughed. It was wonderful to speak to Micheál. She hadn't realised how much she had missed him. He was part of her, somehow, and it was not just the absence of the other Irishman in her life that had produced the empty feeling inside her.

'I'm coming to Finland. I have to see you, to make sure you are really okay. Can you get a few days off work, if I come over?' Micheál asked with urgency.

'I suppose I could – I haven't taken many holidays since I got back. When were you thinking of coming?' Hanna was taken aback.

‘As soon as possible! Today if I can – definitely tomorrow, at the latest.’ Micheál was nearly shouting into the phone.

‘Oh, Micheál – I’ve missed your energy!’ said Hanna. ‘Just let me know when you are coming, and I’ll come and collect you from Helsinki airport.’

‘I’ll go searching for flights straight away. I’ll call you back soon. I love you!’

‘I love you too, Micheál. I’m looking forward to seeing you.’

*

Hanna hadn’t felt so good since leaving Ireland. She impatiently scanned the faces of the arriving passengers, waiting to spot the familiar features of her best friend. There was a warm glow in her chest, and she couldn’t stop smiling. Butterflies were doing somersaults in her belly, and her overall being felt light. Her darling Micheál was coming to see her!

Hanna had begun to believe it was impossible to have any of her Irish life existing within her Finnish one – but now it seemed that she could at least have Micheál back. He was so dear to her. He had touched her heart in a way that not many had before. It was like finding her missing twin – albeit a mad, Irish one.

And there he was now, rushing towards her with his signature swagger, pushing a massive trolley. In another moment, he had enveloped Hanna in a tight hug that pushed all the air out of her lungs, but she didn't care.

'Oh, I've missed you so much, how could you abandon me so?' Micheál's voice was full of emotion. Tears ran freely down his face. Hanna was also weeping, but – for a change –with happiness.

'I can't believe you are here,' Hanna managed to say, once she had caught her breath and blown her nose.

'Let's get out of here. I've so much to talk to you about,' Micheál exclaimed, and ushered Hanna out into the chilly April evening. He did a doubletake when he saw the snow on the ground, literally skidding to a halt in his fancy shoes.

'Oh, yes – we've still got snow. Toughest winter in, like, forever. Just walk slowly so that you don't fall. My car is over there.' Hanna pointed, ploughing ahead at a terrifying pace, at least in Micheál's opinion. He followed her gingerly, taking tiny little steps.

'Hurry up, it's freezing!'

'Ah, come on! One minute you're telling me to go slow, the next to hurry up. You really are an awfully bossy woman,' Micheál shot back.

'Oh, Micheál – I've missed you.'

'Oh, me too – you have no idea how much.'

*

'Now, that's better!' Micheál collapsed onto Hanna's oversized sofa. 'Those flights were murder. I never knew it was so difficult to get anywhere. Sure, I was sent all over the place – I don't even remember how many countries I visited today.'

'Oh, stop your drama,' scoffed Hanna. 'You only had a stopover in Copenhagen, and that's a really lovely airport.'

'I suppose so, but I'm still tired. Enough about me. Tell me, girl – what on earth happened? Why did you abandon us all so suddenly and so cruelly?'

'Ouch, you want to discuss that so soon... it's still very difficult for me to talk about. I haven't spoken of it to anyone.'

'Well, then – it's about time to start.'

Hanna sighed. It seemed obvious that Micheál was not going to drop the subject. She had hoped that they could talk about it much later – or preferably never. She sat down in one of her 1930s armchairs.

'Sebastian is a bastard – a dishonest, two-timing bastard. He was going out with that PA of his, Cathy.'

'What? I don't believe it!' Micheál practically leapt out of his seat, he was so shocked. He hadn't expected to hear that. 'No, I don't buy it – not Sebastian?'

'It's true. Cathy said it was over before we got together, but I don't believe it. And Cathy was pregnant with his child. It's probably born now and everything.'

Hanna's face got tighter and tighter by the second, her arms crossed against her chest. She was furious.

'That can't be right. How did you find out?'

'Cathy came to see me the night before I left. She told me about the baby. She told me that she and Sebastian had been planning to tell me about her being pregnant. How could he do that? I mean, one minute have sex with her and the next with me – and he had me convinced that he cared for me! Cathy said that Sebastian was supposed to tell me the last time I saw him, that day in his office. You remember that day, don't you? It was the last time I saw you, too. Cathy came to see me just after you left that evening and told me everything. She'd felt guilty about it all, and wanted to clear her conscience. She said that she'd asked Sebastian if he'd told me that day, and when he said "no", she felt she had to break it to me. Sebastian said to go ahead, he didn't think I'd care. I just can't believe it. *Not care*! Of course I *cared* that he'd got his PA pregnant! What kind of a sicko is able to do that?'

Hanna was screaming now, all the pent-up anger and resentment at last able to find a voice. She badly wanted to hit something. The next minute, tears of frustration were flowing again.

Micheál was up off his seat in a flash.

'Oh, you poor thing! Come here, now – I'll look after you,' he said, enveloping Hanna yet again in a big hug. Hanna let herself be led to the sofa, where she cried like she had never yet cried, while Micheál murmured, 'That's it, let it all out.'

After a long while, Hanna's sobs grew softer and further apart. Micheál's shirt was completely ruined, but he didn't care. He was usually very particular about his clothes, but he just couldn't get over the amazing feeling of having Hanna back in his life.

Gone at last were those awful nights of sitting at home, brooding over having lost her, never feeling quite right. Lately, Micheál had got into the bad habit of hitting the whisky bottle late in the evening when he had missed Hanna the most. His apartment was trendy and minimalist, with floor-to-ceiling windows looking out over the River Liffey. He had always loved it, and its simple yet elegant furnishings, but in the past few months since Hanna's departure, he had felt like a caged animal. Yet he was sick of going out. Everyone was so fabulously done up, with air kisses and exclamations of "Dahling!" flying around. He had lost his mojo, his muse, his *je ne sais quoi.* And he knew that really what he was missing was Hanna.

And here she was now. Broken-hearted, blotchy-faced, beautiful Hanna – his Hanna. And he was never going to let her go again.

## Chapter 12

Sofia loved having Aaron around. Once the time allowed by his travel visa had run out, Sofia made sure to apply for a work visa for him, in order for him to continue at the stables as long as he liked.

Aaron was a natural with her horses. He had a way about him that was irresistible to anyone, human or animal. Sofia was incredibly taken with him. He got up first thing in the morning, even earlier than Sofia, his relaxed whistling waking her as he swept the yard outside her window, filled up the water buckets for the horses, or fed the dogs. She received the brightest welcome from him every morning when she arrived in the yard, and she couldn't wait to see him each day. There was nothing like his sunny disposition to put a permanent smile on a girl's face.

Sofia was discovering new facets to herself in Aaron's company. Many a time she would be content just to stand still and lean on a pitchfork, listening to his stories of life on his father's family ranch, nestled in hundreds of acres of Australian bush, where they had horses, sheep and plenty of wildlife. He'd spend a long time describing what it was like to walk in the bush. Sofia never stood or sat down without doing something, but there was something about Aaron that put her into a trance and allowed her to stop, relax and enjoy the moments she shared with him.

It was yet another such wonderful morning when Sofia found herself enthralled by Aaron's accent and his stories while getting the horses' breakfasts ready. She was moving at a snail's pace, willing the moment to last as long as possible.

'And what about you, Sofia? Why are you living in Ireland and not in Finland?' For the first time, Aaron challenged their non-verbal agreement by asking a personal question. It was such a simple thing, but Sofia was rattled. She had let her guard down and now she didn't know what to do. She wanted to tell him, an urge that she had never felt before. Sofia never talked about herself, never explained her background or thoughts to anyone, unless it was something related to the business. But now she found herself thinking, *why not*?

Sofia realised that she wanted to continue talking to this man, that she wanted to talk to him again tomorrow, and the day after. Suddenly that was much more important than anything else. 'I came here to work with horses, and then an opportunity arose for me to get my own stables, so here I am.' *That wasn't so hard now, was it?*

'Ace – a bit like myself, then, in a way. Here I came, and here I stayed. And how long have you been here, then?'

'Ten years.' It was getting easier, although she didn't know how to elaborate.

‘And will you tell me about Finland sometime? What is it like? I know nothing about it, but I’m fascinated. You only ever hear good things about it – or crazy things.’

Aaron was looking at Sofia intently, gauging her reaction. He looked a bit nervous, very unlike him. Sofia smiled at him, indicating that it was all right, that she welcomed the new direction their perfect working relationship was taking.

‘I’d love to tell you about Finland. Haven’t thought about the place for quite some time, so it would be nice to do so. How about tonight? I have a special place higher up on the mountain I like to go sometimes. We could bring a bottle of wine...’ Sofia couldn’t believe this was coming out of her mouth, but then again, everything in relation to Aaron always surprised her. Another pearl on the long string of firsts. She had no idea what was coming, scaring her witless. She always planned everything very carefully. Nothing about anything with Aaron had been planned – and she loved everything about it.

‘Ace! That sounds like a plan!’ Aaron flashed his lazy smile, one side of his mouth going up more than the other, a motion so familiar and dear to Sofia.

She couldn’t wait for the evening.

*

Tim was sweating buckets. This was the most important gig of his life. Not because it would make any great difference to his musical career – it was just a simple four-man set, in a nice pub in Temple Bar. It was important because this was the night he had been dreaming about for a long time. Cathy would hear him play the guitar at last.

It had taken him months to build up his courage to ask Sebastian to bring Cathy to hear him play. Not for the lack of gigs – he was doing better than ever. He had been asked to play with some great bands; even the Chieftains had asked him to work with them, and he'd done a fair bit of touring too. But it was time to make something good happen – or so he hoped. Surely Cathy would melt at the sound of his passionate playing, as so many women had over the years? *Off to the gig, then. If I'm able to play, that is. The way I'm feeling now it would be no wonder if I threw up halfway through.*

Cathy, meanwhile, was overjoyed that Sebastian had finally asked her out. She had thoroughly enjoyed her favourite pizza in Milano's that evening. It wasn't the first time they had gone there together, but this felt different. Firstly, they had not gone straight from work, but at eight in the evening, meaning they had both gone home to change. And afterwards, Sebastian had brought her along to a gig by a friend of his, which sounded very much like a proper date. Sebastian had looked so forlorn for many months now – in fact, since Hanna had gone – and Cathy had sometimes nearly felt guilty. But the old Sebastian had been back today when he had asked her out. Things were definitely looking up for her.

Sebastian felt delighted with himself. Tim's plan was coming together, and Sebastian wished with his entire being that his good friend would at last be successful with Cathy. Tim was a good lad and deserved every bit of happiness, and if he wanted Cathy, then Sebastian would do all in his power to help him.

'Hiya, folks! Good to be here again. Hope you like the tunes we have for you tonight. The first one is from Donegal and called the – ah, what was it now? Something "Priest" – Tim, I've forgotten. Help me out here.'

'Sorry, mate, can't help you,' Tim flung back. 'I'm a Dub!'

'Ah, whatever it's called – enjoy it, now.'

The band launched into an upbeat Irish piece, to loud cheers from the audience. Cathy couldn't believe her eyes. It was him – Tim, the cameraman. The bumbling idiot who had thankfully been absent lately from the office. She looked over at Sebastian, and saw confirmation in his eyes. He was beaming, pointing at Tim with a thumbs-up over the loud music.

Cathy was thoroughly confused. Why would Sebastian want to listen to Tim on their date? Did he not understand that Cathy couldn't stand the guy? Perhaps he had never properly understood her frowns and scowls when Tim was around. Not much of a date. Although, she had to admit, the music was good.

'He's great, isn't he?' Sebastian shouted into her ear.

Cathy turned to look at Tim properly for the first time. He wasn't at all the same clumsy idiot that she saw around the office. He looked almost… graceful. His permanent grin was present as ever, but his body was lithe, and moved to the rhythm of his energetic strumming.

'Not bad,' Cathy admitted, more to herself than to Sebastian. She was surprised, and not too many things surprised her in life. 'Not bad at all.'

Seeing the astonished look on Cathy's face, Sebastian began to feel hopeful for his friend. Perhaps Cathy could be brought around after all.

Cathy had always been irritated by Tim's cheery nature – mostly because she felt that his presence was a distraction, and an obstacle to her being alone with Sebastian. Yet tonight, she felt something different. For the first time, she began to understand Tim, and to feel the infectiousness of his good cheer. 'He really can play,' she yelled to Sebastian.

Sebastian hugged Cathy spontaneously. She always had a smile for him, but the rest of the time she went around the office wearing a frown, always irked by "idiots" – i.e. anyone that annoyed her or thwarted her efficient ways as she bent the world to her will. It was good to see her smile – her face looked softer.

Tim played as if his life depended on it, channelling all of his nervous energy into his performance. He felt the music flow through him and out through his fingertips as he furiously willed the guitar to do his bidding. And it sounded pretty special. *If this doesn't melt her ice, nothing ever will*, he thought. The other lads followed his lead, playing their way to their best gig in a long time. And the audience loved it – they were going wild as the band's infectious excitement spread through the room.

Cathy could not take her eyes off Tim. She even forgot about Sebastian at times – despite the fact that this was supposed to have been the culmination of all her efforts over the years: The Date.

Tim noticed to his delight that Cathy was smiling at him. She had acknowledged him! His fingers felt removed from his body as they joyfully jumped up and down the neck and body of the guitar, so fast they were going. He had a chance now. She obviously liked what he did: his music, the most important thing in his life. And she looked so pretty tonight. *Thanks, Seb!* Tim thought.

Cathy had to admit that Sebastian had not treated her any differently tonight than at any other time. Even the entertainment was being provided by another employee of his company – more like a work do than a date. *He was never going to love me*, Cathy realised. Her shoulders slumped with the force of the revelation. All her hard work over the years to lure him in was for nothing. But before she gave up on Sebastian completely, she had to know for sure.

'Um, Sebastian. Can I just ask you something? At the back, where it's not so noisy.'

'Sure, but – do you not want to hear some more?'

'I do – it's fantastic – but I really need to ask you something quickly.'

'Sure.'

They headed through the back doors to find a quiet corner.

Cathy took a deep breath. 'Sebastian. Do you think you could ever develop – how can I say this? – romantic feelings for me?'

Sebastian was completely taken aback. He had suspected that Cathy's devotion to him was a little more than professional pride, but since he couldn't reciprocate, he had ignored those thoughts. A mistake, obviously. And here she was now, looking at him, asking him straight out. While he would never love Cathy in the way that she wanted, he couldn't bear to hurt her feelings, after all they had been through together. She was too important to him, not to mention to his business. He took a deep breath.

'I'm so sorry, Cathy. You know I respect and like you enormously – but if I had any other feelings for you, I'm sure I would have told you years ago.' Sebastian tried to speak as gently as possible in order to lessen the blow. He surveyed Cathy's face to gauge the impact his words were having, worried that she was going to crumble, go into hysterics or some other horribly female reaction.

'Not to worry,' replied Cathy, as breezily as she could manage. 'I've been rather silly. I do hope this won't change our working relationship in any way.' So it was as she had suspected, known in fact tonight. He cared for her, but not in the way she had dreamed about. It had all been for nothing. Cathy felt numb.

'Cathy, of course it won't! I couldn't do what I do without you – please don't leave me now.' Sebastian was getting worried. Cathy seemed to be taking it well, though. Maybe it would be all right. He certainly wished it would be so – that they could move on and forget this awkward moment as fast as possible.

'Oh, Sebastian. I would never leave you. I truly respect you, and believe in what you do. And I love working for you. Let's go back inside and hear Tim play some more.' Cathy was able to give Sebastian a small smile. And she wanted to see Tim. Such an interesting thought, something she could have never believed in a million years.

Cathy felt bruised by their conversation. On one level, it had been horrific. She had never been one to share her emotions freely. And to be rejected… But she also felt relieved. It seemed that a chapter of her life was ending, a hard chapter of long years of unrequited love. Or whatever it had been – she wasn't sure. Yet she felt a wonder, a curious lightness that she didn't have to care about Sebastian so much any more. She didn't have to analyse every little word, every gesture of his to see if it contained hidden meanings about his feelings for her. She didn't need to plot and plan how to win his heart. That had all been such hard work, and she no longer had to do any of it. Cathy felt lighter. Her feelings for Sebastian had been suffocating her, weighing her down for years.

'Yes, let's go.' Sebastian felt relieved. It obviously wasn't as serious as he had thought if she was able to smile. And she wanted to hear Tim again. That was good news for his buddy.

*

Cathy was having the first true crisis of her life.

She had been restless all day – for several days now, in fact, but today she felt particularly uncomfortable, as it was a Saturday and there was no work there to distract her. She had been pacing around her apartment in Temple Bar for quite some time, her inability to decide a course of action unnerving her almost as much as the alien feeling.

She felt guilty, which was something she had never felt before. Had she messed up Sebastian's chance for happiness with Hanna in her mistaken quest for his heart? After she had admitted to herself that Sebastian was never going to love her romantically, she had felt numb for days. It was as if everything in her life had to be reorganised, since her focus was no longer Sebastian.

On the one hand, she felt relieved that she didn't have to try so hard any more. She didn't have to capture Sebastian's attention, nor did she have to figure out any more what Sebastian's dream woman was like, and try to be that woman. All those endless hours – years – of speculation, planning and dreaming were over.

On the other hand, she felt empty. What was it all for now? What was there to look forward to, since she didn't have Sebastian to chase after any longer? Her entire life had been built around Sebastian, her love and longing for him and for a relationship with him. Cathy still cared about him a lot – but to her surprise, she could see that she no longer loved him in that desperate way, that always hurt and pushed her to try to be better for him. In her mind, Cathy had built Sebastian into an unattainable superman. And what did that say about her beliefs about a relationship? Had she heard nothing Sebastian had taught her?

Sebastian would ask her, if he was here now: what was the reason for her to continue to believe so long in the idea that he would suddenly start loving her passionately and declare himself to her? She could see now that her whole way of thinking had been very wrong. But then, that was the nature of negative beliefs, Cathy reminded herself. *Once the negative belief no longer holds power over you, it appears totally ludicrous*. She had been listening to Sebastian for years but had always felt that she was beyond needing to develop herself – that she was pretty perfect. What had made her hold onto those strange ideas for so long?

Something had happened inside her in that moment in the pub. Listening to Tim playing in so heavenly a fashion, it was as if she had snapped out of a long daze – as if a fog had been cleared away from her eyes. Sebastian didn't love her. Cathy's mind was whirling. She found herself thinking about how Tim looked when he was playing, of the pure joy in his face. Cathy didn't think she had ever felt such happiness in her life.

Cathy had not had many romantic relationships, preferring to focus on her career. She had to admit that she had no idea what a real relationship would look like. She had only ever dated men who could benefit her career in some way. There had never been any passion. Even Sebastian fitted the mould: her very own action hero, someone she would be proud to bring home due to his outstanding success. So what were the ingredients of a good relationship? And where on earth had she picked up these beliefs about a relationship equalling compatible work practices?

Cathy sat down on her sofa and sighed heavily. Her head, normally so organised, was full of strange thoughts today, making her feel nauseated. She lay down and closed her eyes, hoping that it would help her calm down. Yet another first: the Cathy of old would never have considered lying down in the afternoon.

Images floated before her eyes: her mother and father, sitting rigidly at the dinner table, as they gave guidance to their children about proper etiquette, preparing them to dine out or host their own dinner parties. Cathy remembered feeling in such awe of her beautiful mother and well-groomed father. She had always tried her very best to please them. And what was their relationship like? They had both worked at a high level in the civil service – *very compatible careers, then*, Cathy thought. They had never shown much affection to each other in front of the children, apart from a polite peck on the cheek, as was proper and expected. *So no great passion there, as far as I know*, thought Cathy, ticking the points off her mental list. No wonder she had always felt that the other girls in her boarding school were extremely silly, mooning over some pop star or the young men in the boys' boarding school nearby. She had never seen evidence of passionate love in the relationship between the two people that she had admired most all her life: her parents.

No great surprise, then, that she had never thought Sebastian's lack of passion for her was an obstacle to their relationship. She had even regarded Sebastian's little affair with that Finnish girl as a passing fancy, nothing true nor lasting – although the fact that it had dragged on a little had started to worry her towards the end, which is one of the reasons why she had decided to act.

She would have to think about this some more, she decided. But not today – her head was starting to ache. And under no circumstances was she going to tell Sebastian what she had done. At best, he would fire her, and then where would she be?

Cathy felt exhausted. She closed her eyes. Perhaps she would be able to sleep a little, to get out of her head for a bit, and stop her heart aching so much. She would try.

*

Sebastian was back in Dublin, giving yet another speech. It felt good to be back on stage. Work was good, and he enjoyed it as much as ever. And yet, he was still lonely. Nobody seemed to compare to his Hanna. He still missed her, although it was now more like a dull ache than a constant pain. He was lonely, and there seemed to be nothing he could do about it except hope that one day things might change.

Sebastian sighed deeply as he listened to Cathy's final remarks introducing him and his genius to the audience. Cathy's loyalty to him was touching. She seemed to have been extra nice to him recently.

Sebastian strode onto the stage. It did feel good. He liked sharing his understanding of the way reality *really* worked, and seeing the wonderment in his audience's eyes as he explained it all. *At least I have my amazing work*, Sebastian thought to himself, feeling appreciation swim through him, letting him breathe easy for a few moments.

After his opening remarks and a few light jokes to set the mood, Sebastian got onto today's topic.

'Now, why am I sometimes called "the Emotions Guy" in the media? Bcause I talk about our emotions – what they are, and what they mean. What are our emotions, feelings? All feelings are secondary responses to something we believe to be true.' *Like, I'm miserable, because I believe Hanna doesn't love me, never did.* Sebastian was finding it hard to muster enthusiasm for his topic since his own heart was aching, badly.

'So, when you're feeling something, it is not your feelings that are the key issue. They are simply a response to your beliefs, indicators on the scale: from believing all is well – a positive feeling – to believing that you are inadequate in some way, and can't do, be, have what you want – a negative feeling.' *I wasn't good enough for her to love me, and I'm miserable still, after all this time.*

'When you feel happy and positive, you believe in your own power to create your life as you want it to be. When you feel bad or negative, you are buying into a limiting belief, one that states that you are not good enough. This should get you immediately into detective mode. Discover what it is you believe that is preventing you from fulfilling your true potential.' *But it is so hard to believe that all is going to be all right, that I have the power to create my life as I want it, when I feel so bad.*

'I'm going to outline a few simple steps to getting in touch with the definitions that are messing up your life. First: be more in tune with your emotions, particularly your negative ones. Very often, when you are dealing with a long-standing limiting belief, you become accustomed to the negative feeling attached to it, and don't even realise you are feeling bad. Start focusing on your feelings. Watch for them – notice when you are not feeling good.' *This is such an easy step, as I feel miserable all the time*. Sebastian sighed heavily. Hanna's image was in front of his eyes constantly, tormenting him.

'Second, remind yourself that your feelings are merely responses to your beliefs. When you become aware of a negative feeling, stop and close your eyes. Ask yourself: I'm feeling a negative emotion; what is it that I'm thinking about right now?

'The little voice in our heads narrates our lives continuously. We are so accustomed to it, we rarely even hear what it is saying. So the second step is to become aware of this little voice.

'The third step is to take a pen and paper, and start writing down the beliefs that your little voice produces when you are feeling a negative emotion. Let's say that you are, in your opinion, a bit overweight, and you think you should lose some weight. It's evening, and you're home, feeling a bit bored and dissatisfied. Remember, the first step is to notice this negative feeling.

'You plonk yourself down on the sofa, close your eyes and you tune into your little voice. It's having a little merry-go-round chat on your favourite subject for beating yourself up about – your weight. It's saying things like, "Oh, I'm bored. I want to eat some chocolate, but I can't have it because I'll just get fatter. And then I'll hate myself even more... why can't I eat everything I want? It's not fair... I just want some chocolate... No, you can't have it, it's bad for you... You are a fat slob, you should go to the gym... You're so fat... You'll never be thin..." Write it all down, even if it makes you feel a little nauseated – and there you'll have your beliefs about your weight issue – at least some of them.

'The fourth step is to start analysing these beliefs. Sounds scary, right? Actually, this is pretty straightforward – and if you do it, you'll soon feel much better, so this is the nicest step. Keep the pen and paper handy, as you may find there are more beliefs to be discovered as you go.

'Ask yourself: how does it serve me to believe this? Why do I believe it? What do I fear so much that this awful alternative seems better? Why do I define it negatively?' *Indeed, so simple, yet so difficult. If only I could answer this question myself. I've found many answers to these questions already, but none of them seem to help, none of them seem to give me the relief I need.*

'Remember, you are always 100% motivated away from pain. In this case, you have already chosen the belief that you see as less painful than the one that you really fear.

'In the case of our weight-issue girl, she has chosen to say to herself that she's a "fat slob". The Big Scary Belief behind this could be, for example, that "I am just no good as a human being, nobody can love me, least of all myself, because I can't even control what I eat". Your beliefs are always personal. But what I do know is that they are not aligned with your true self, which is good and pure – and that is why you experience the negative feeling.

'Discovering your negative beliefs is something that you have to do yourself. Just remember, that when you are feeling that negative emotion, and you begin digging up your beliefs, and you recognise *why* you are doing something, you have already changed it. All you have to do is to realise that you are choosing it for a reason, and when you no longer buy into that reason, it's gone.' *But I still believe I wasn't good enough for Hanna. She hates me now, and I don't know why. I can't imagine ever caring for someone else. She was special. And I was not special enough.*

Sebastian finished up with a few closing remarks, and took a bow to a standing ovation. The audience had lapped it up as usual. Sebastian chatted with many of them after the speech, but he was relieved when he was finally able to get into his car and drive home. The buzz of the speech had worn off and he was tired again. His chest was tight, and he felt unbearably lonely.

Sebastian pulled up outside his apartment complex and went in. His own words were still swirling around in his head, and he decided yet again to sit down and to take out his notebook, already filled with pages and pages of his feelings about losing Hanna. He had made it sound so easy in his speech: just four little steps to sorting out one's issues. But he knew that his loss of Hanna was not an easy one to resolve.

It had been useful, though. He had unearthed a lot of old beliefs he had about relationships. He took his pen and paper again, and started writing. He wrote about trying to treat Hanna with the utmost respect, giving her lots of space to get used to being with him. But it didn't feel good. He realised that he was picking up a feeling of anxiety that had always accompanied his desire to be kind. Why had he been so nervous about her?

And suddenly, he knew. He hadn't been nervous about her reaction but about his own. He had always held back because he didn't want to become a monster. Before Hanna, he had always ended relationships before they had even really got going. He now realised that he had always believed that a man in a relationship was inherently going to turn into a nasty caveman of a tyrant, ruling every aspect of the woman's life, and he had never wanted to be that man. He didn't want to control Hanna's life – he just wanted to share it. He wanted to be a loving partner, always there for her, not a jealous monster.

How on earth had he believed that a man in a relationship is always the boss, the worst kind that enslaved the other person? He had paid lip-service to the idea of an equal partnership – he had never really believed it was possible. How on earth did he have a belief like that, a belief he had never noticed before, a belief that had been hidden away so deeply that he had no idea it was lurking in his mind? Sebastian knew. The fear he had experienced was that of turning into his father if he ever he got deeper into a relationship. That he would become a demanding, overpowering jerk.

For the first time, Sebastian was able to confront his view of his father as a terrible man, and recognise in it his own distorted belief. It was a belief not shared by his mother, he realised. She adored Sebastian's father, and always had. As he explored his feelings, Sebastian saw that he had projected his beliefs about his relationship with his father onto his mother, and onto all of his own relationships. His dad had always been an awful tyrant with him, forever ordering him around, trying either to put him down or to bully him into doing things his way.

And now he could see that his dad was nothing like that with his mother. Athough Sebastian's mum gave the impression that Gerald was in charge, Sebastian could now bring to mind evidence that his dad always watched Eileen very carefully when he was making some decision or another for both of them; often he had changed his mind suddenly, which irritated Sebastian. But now he could see that his mum must have been giving his dad non-verbal messages. So his dad did take his mum's point of view into account. How had Sebastian missed that? It was so obvious to him now. His father was not a monster in his own relationship.

Just like that, it was over.

Sebastian felt light-headed with the relief flooding his body. He searched inside himself, and found that the negative feelings towards his father were gone. His mother loved his dad. She thought he was great. He was a good man, and not the monster Sebastian had made him out to be.

Now he could see that he had handled his relationship with Hanna all wrong. He'd been too reticent with her. Had he ever even told her that he loved her? He had wanted to give Hanna all the time and space she needed to get used to the idea of them having a life together, but this kindness had been unwittingly created from the negative – from his fear of turning into his father – or rather, from his fear of turning into such a man as he imagined his father to be: an overpowering buffoon. Just as clearly, he now knew that his father was not the man he had imagined. He was a caring family man, but he didn't know how to relate to his only son. But Sebastian could change this now, since he had unearthed an inkling of what was actually going on. He had a strong feeling that his relationship with his dad was going to change for the better. And it felt great.

So what did this mean in relation to Hanna? Had Hanna known that he absolutely adored her? He didn't think so. He had been blind to his own failings, and now he regretted it deeply. If he had lost Hanna because of his misguided relationship with his father... the thought terrified Sebastian.

Fundamentally, he still believed that Hanna had been the one for him. But something was bothering him about the way she had departed. He couldn't understand how it had all gone so wrong, and so quickly. One minute she had been there, obviously very much in love with him, and the next minute she had turned into a screaming banshee and run off, leaving him to lick his wounds. He felt like a private investigator of his own relationship: there was a huge clue just sitting there, right in front of his nose, that he was somehow unable to see.

## Chapter 13

Micheál had practically moved in with Hanna, working his business in Ireland over the phone, via Skype and through a stream of emails. He had even begun to sleep in her double bed with her, rather than on her sofa. And he loved Finland. He threw himself into studying the language, buying up cratefuls of books and tapes, and he had Hanna going through his lessons with him every night. He progressed pretty well, even though Finnish seemed like such a difficult language. As impossible as the people, but yet so fascinating, thought Micheál. He was already able to have simple conversations in Finnish, ordering meals and asking for directions. And he was getting to know Helsinki, forever harassing the locals for conversational opportunities.

The horrible snow had thankfully disappeared within two weeks of his arrival, with the advent of the spring sunshine, and there had only been a handful of overcast or rainy days since. This made his daily wandering around the city centre a much easier task. The temperature had also started to creep up, even hitting double figures occasionally during the day.

Hanna and Micheál had celebrated *vappu*, the eve of the first of May, in true Finnish style, hitting the town with everyone else. Hanna had managed to get Micheál one of the sailor-style secondary school graduation caps, and he had gone around with the hoards of young Finns shouting '*hyvää vappua!*', and draped in colourful party stuff. He had loved the taste of *sima*, a homebrew of sugar, water, lemons and raisins, and stuffed his face with homemade ring donuts, which he had sugared himself.

He loved his new life. He was never going back to Ireland. He would stay with Hanna and live his happy-ever-after in Finland.

Hanna was also delighted beyond words to have Micheál back in her life. It helped alleviate the ache of Sebastian's absence so much that she hardly ever thought about him anymore. She had learned to accept that he was gone, and that she had to find a way to get on with the rest of her life. And with Micheál by her side, that was looking considerably easier. He brought with him a strong flavour of the spirit of Ireland that she had missed so much: he never sat still unless absolutely necessary and talked non-stop until he literally collapsed into bed out of sheer exhaustion.

Hanna called her mother.

'*Äiti*? I have my Irish friend Micheál staying with me at the moment, and I'd like to bring him down to show him where I grew up. I was thinking about next weekend. Are you around then?'

'Yes, we are here. We were going to go to the summer cottage. When were you coming?'

'We were thinking of coming on Friday night after I finish work, which means we should be there around 7 o'clock.'

'Okay, that would be fine. I could make some food. What does your friend like? Would he eat some pork chops?'

'Yes, he loves them!'

'That's good. Why don't I ask Miia to come down also with her family? Are you planning to stay the weekend?'

'Yes, we are. We were going to visit the summer cottage also, but maybe just during the day on Saturday.'

'Good. We'll go down to the cottage late on Friday evening, to give you some peace and quiet, and you can then come over on Saturday, when you are ready, and go back to the city when you've had enough. I think we could even get the barbecue going on Saturday – the weather is supposed to be good.'

'Oh, great – we'll see you on Friday evening, then.'

'Yes, see you then!'

*Well, that's that sorted*, Hanna thought happily. Her mind was busily planning all the places she would show Micheál when they got to Turku. Friday evening would be spent with her family, but on Saturday morning she could take him into the city centre, and then maybe she'd show him the cathedral by the *River Aura*, and perhaps also the castle closer to the sea... there were so many possibilities.

But before they went, Hanna decided to buy herself a car. She had got rid of her old one when she got the concert hall job. She lived only a few minutes by bus or tram from the city, and it was just as easy to get around by public transport as it was by car. She had grown so tired of the fact that cars required so much maintenance in the winter time, from the changing of tyres to windows requiring constant scraping of ice and brushing off of snow.

But now there were two of them to consider – her own little family. Micheál had indicated that he was in no hurry to go back to Ireland, and Hanna was very glad to let him stay in her place indefinitely. In fact, the thought of him going back filled her with horror.

Hanna and Micheál had a good hunt on the Internet, and settled on a little Toyota Yaris. It was a private sale, and the owner had promised to bring it down to show them. Neither Hanna nor Micheál knew anything about cars, but the seller had proclaimed himself to be a bit of a wizard, explaining how he had serviced this, that and the other. He assured them that it was all in top condition – and the car was red, Hanna's favourite colour.

'See this gasket here: I've replaced it only recently, as well as this valve here and that...' the seller droned. Hanna had stopped listening a long time ago as none of it made any sense to her. All she understood was that the car looked good on the outside as well as on the inside, and it felt fine when she drove it. She wished the guy would stop talking so that she could give him the money and tell him to go home. Micheál, meanwhile, was listening carefully, trying to understand as many words as possible. There seemed to be a lot of technical jargon thrown in, and it was obvious to him that Hanna had tuned out, staring happily at the car. But the seller had a clear speaking voice and didn't rush his words, making the task of understanding him a lot easier for Micheál – even though he didn't really know most of the words. The sound of the language was becoming a lot more familiar, and he was now well able to make out where one word stopped and the next one started, although the meanings were still hazy.

But what a fascinating language! Nothing like any of the two European languages he had lazily studied in school: Irish and French. The grammar was pretty much attached as suffixes at the end of the words. Ironically, the emphasis was always at the start of the word. Most Finns sounded like they had run out of air, energy, or both, by the end of a word – where all the most important information was located. The Finns themselves didn't seem to have any difficulty understanding this contradictory way of speaking, so Micheál just had to keep at it, practising and listening as much as possible. He was convinced that he'd get there. Eventually.

The seller finished his monologue at last. Maybe he had noticed that his audience wasn't as riveted as him about the information he was spewing out, or perhaps he was satisfied that he had told them everything they would ever need to know, thus rendering his liability on any future claims null and void. Whatever the reason, he turned to Hanna and asked her if there was a deal to be made.

'Yes, I'll take it,' Hanna said enthusiastically. She was buying a car! She could take some time off in a few weeks when the summer got properly under way and they could go on a roadtrip. Hanna was so busy dreaming up holiday scenarios that Micheál had to grab her hand to get her back to the moment, so that she could hand over the money and they could get motoring.

*

Micheál was scared. Driving on the wrong side of the road – or the right side, according to the Finns – was a terrifying experience. He had never before driven on the right, and it was disconcerting to have the cars coming at you. Turning off was a total nightmare: he never had any idea where he was supposed to go. And Hanna screaming, 'Go left' or 'Go right, right!' didn't help one bit – he had always been totally confused by the concepts of left and right. Driving in Ireland, left was easy and right was more difficult, as turning right meant crossing the traffic – but this system didn't work in Finland. His brain was scrambled.

Luckily, they were only out to take a quick spin in Hanna's new car the night after buying it, and Micheál could cut short this terrifying experience. It was mutually concluded that Hanna would do all the driving from now on.

The weather had turned gorgeous. Finland did occasionally get the first heatwave of summer during the second half of May, and this year they were lucky. The temperature soared to 25 degrees Celsius. Hanna dug out her summer clothes, and they dashed to the shops to buy Micheál a new summer wardrobe. Hanna's storage space was beginning to get tight, with Micheál's stuff starting to clutter up her little apartment. He had mainly brought spring clothes, but now he needed shorts, sandals, sleeveless shirts, summer hats and accessories. He had to look his best to impress Hanna's family.

On Friday, Hanna finished work a little earlier than usual and rushed home so that they could get going. Micheál had been busy all morning packing for them, rummaging through Hanna's wardrobe to see what treasures were hidden there. He packed her bag for her also, having made the best choices out of a slightly depressing collection, resolving as he did so to take Hanna out shopping as soon as possible. How had he never noticed that most of her clothes were awful? She was a good-looking woman, but a lot could be done to enhance her appearance further by improving her wardrobe. *That will have to wait until we come back from visiting the folks*, he thought.

The drive to Turku would only take about an hour and half, since the new motorway had opened up only a few years previously. Hanna was curious to drive on it, as she had usually taken the train to Turku when visiting her family. Micheál learned that there were many long tunnels on the road that had cost a fortune to build, and that the construction had been delayed for years, as an endangered species of flying squirrel had been discovered en route. All Micheál could see were endless amount of trees everywhere, dotted with the occasional lake and some fields. No people anywhere.Trees, trees and trees: no wonder Hanna had always been so shocked in Ireland by their absence.

*

Hanna and Micheál were relaxing in the late evening sunshine on the terrace outside Hanna's parents' summer cottage. Their bellies were full to bursting with Hanna's mother's delicious barbecue food. There had been fried potatoes and lots of salads, marinated pork chops and chicken, and of course, enormous Finnish sausages. Micheál had been upset that he hadn't had a chance to try the customary method of cooking these, on sticks over the fire. Hanna assured him, however, that he'd get his chance to do so later – if he could ever eat again, that is.

After the long and hard winter, it could seem to take forever for spring to get going in Finland – and then suddenly, with the arrival of a bit of fine weather, it all happened at once. Nature burst forth in her full glory. The birch trees were in leaf, their lovely pale branches moving gently in the light breeze. The Finns had a love affair with the birch, delighting in the contrast the slender trees created with the dark greens of pine and spruce. The birches returned their love by growing everywhere in great numbers.

Hanna and Micheál were enjoying their time with Hanna's family. They had arrived at Hanna's parents' house the previous day, and had a city garden barbecue together with Hanna's sister's family. Miia, Jukka and little Suvi had also joined them at the summer cottage, and the day had been spent playing traditional games. Suvi kept them all entertained with her toddler antics, waddling around the garden in delight at her newfound ability to walk. The little darling had collapsed onto her bed straight after dinner, having first performed an excellent impression of an old drunkard passing out at the dinner table, her head nodding as she bravely tried to stay awake as long as possible.

Hanna's parents had been slightly surprised at Micheál's unexpected command of Finnish. They were themselves of the generation of Finns that had not learned English at school, and Micheál's efforts made communication a great deal easier. Not that much had been said above and beyond some small talk about the weather and the food: they mostly left Hanna and Micheál to keep their own company.

Micheál had asked Hanna if she thought they approved of him, as they didn't really try to speak with him. Hanna assured him that yes, they did seem to like him well enough, and that leaving them well alone was perfectly normal behaviour. *The Finns sure did give one space!* Micheál hadn't really understood what she meant by it until he had experienced it at first hand. Not a bad thing, once you got used to the idea.

'I love Finland so much! I can't believe my luck that I'm able to live here now,' Micheál exclaimed.

Hanna smiled at him. She was amused by Micheál's crush on Finland. She agreed with him that the country was great, but he was in his honeymoon phase, and Hanna knew that the rose-tinted glasses would have to come off at some point. Not that it had all been easy for him – quite the opposite, in fact. The Finns mostly ignored his constant efforts to engage in conversation, usually looking at him as if he had two heads when he tried. His extremely jolly manner was the main cause; Hanna was having a great time observing his attempts to assimilate into the society, while simultaneously changing all of the Finns to be more like him by sheer force of personality. And so often, he was successful in shaking them out of their shells. Never a dull moment with Micheál.

Hanna knew that while she was working, Micheál spent a lot of his time roaming the city, looking for opportunities to talk with people, in order to practise his Finnish and to learn more about the culture. Micheál's brass neck stood him in good stead. It didn't matter to him how many Finns shunned him as a lunatic – he was a man on a mission, and he was going to learn the language and culture as fast as it was humanly possible. Hanna could understand how he had managed to build such a successful events management business in Ireland, as he was no quitter, and did not understand the concept of failure. She was curious to see how long it would take him before he organised his first gig in Finland. She didn't think she'd have to wait long.

'I am truly glad you are here,' Hanna said. 'I was miserable without you.'

'I know, I'm such sunshine, etcetera, etcetera. I know it didn't work out with you-know-who, but I'm here to prove to you that not all Irish men are bastards. I'll never leave you alone – unless of course, you want me to.' Micheál turned to look at Hanna, flooding her with the love that shone from his eyes.

'Micheál, you know I love you. I'd marry you this instant, if only you could give me children. I've been thinking lately that we are such a perfect family, you and I, and the only thing we're missing is kids.'

'Hanna, really? You want to have children? But I never knew.'

'Yes. Look at Suvi. She's so wonderful, isn't she? I want to have that in my life at some point – but I worry that it'll never happen. I'm off "normal" men for life, I think, so I've got a bit of a dilemma...'

'Hanna, if it is children you want, I'll give them to you. You know I would do anything for you.' Micheál was looking at Hanna, holding both of her hands, and for once, being deadly serious.

'Oh, Micheál. Sometimes I wonder about you. Are you sure you are gay?' said Hanna.

'Most definitely, darling. I've never been interested in women – but there is something about you that throws me over the edge. Do you know that I haven't seriously looked at any men since I came to Finland? And there are so many dishy ones here. I'm just too devoted to you.'

'Are you serious about having children?' Hanna looked searchingly at Micheál. The idea had crossed her mind before, and she had always dismissed it as impossible. But something about tonight had pushed her further, and somehow it had just popped out. She must be drunk on delicious food.

'Yes – I am serious. I'm not sure about the logistics of the whole baby-making business just yet, but if you really want them, we'll work something out. I'd like to have the chance to be a father to some gorgeous little Hannas. That's one of the hardest thing about being gay, you know – always knowing that you can't have children. We could be a real family. We could buy a fabulous house in Espoo – you know, one of those ones we saw when we were testing out your car.'

'Oh, Micheál. This could be so perfect.'

Hanna felt charged up, her heart full of this new, unexpected idea. Micheál seemed quiet also, for once, and they both silently contemplated the enormous significance of the direction in which their discussion had taken them.

Hanna was shocked that she had even proposed such a mad scheme to him. Apart from a general feeling she'd always had that one day she would like to have some children, she hadn't been really thinking about having any. With Sebastian, she had begun to believe that their relationship would eventually end up in that happy place where wedding bells and a big house with a family featured, but it had been too early to consider any specific details. Now her faith in the heterosexual male was in tatters, and deep down, she had obviously felt that her chances of ever having children were nil – hence she had blurted out her heart's desire.

*Children.* What a wonderful and scary idea!

Was she ready to take that next step? And with a man she knew she loved deeply, but not romantically? A man that was so obviously gay? A man that would never create the illusion that they were a traditional heterosexual family?

There were many such questions swirling around Hanna's mind, and she was not alone. Micheál likewise was considering this new turn of events. He had long ago given up on the dream of being a father to his own children. But now, here was Hanna, his stunning Hanna, who was willing to give him children and family life in the most beautiful country in the world. Micheál felt awed and overwhelmed. Could he do it? Could he actually get to be a daddy?

What would everybody think of their unconventional family? Would Hanna's parents approve? They seemed like nice people, but who knew? He would hate Hanna to suffer for his sake. And what about the children – would they be mercilessly bullied? And what about him or Hanna finding the man of their dreams? For although Hanna seemed so sure that she was over men for life, that there could be nobody else but Sebastian, there was always a chance that she would meet someone else who was perfect for her. She was so lovely that she wouldn't have any problem attracting men; the question was more one of what she was doing to keep them away. Micheál would hate to stand in the way of her happiness in a normal relationship.

And there was always the question of sex. What about each of them sleeping with other men? How was that supposed to work? Would they agree that they could have all the flings they wanted, but that they'd have to always come home to each other? The questions were endless... It was impossible to tell at this point if

Micheál felt that the benefits of having a great family with Hanna outweighed the problems it would bring. Unconventional was never easy.

Suddenly, Micheál felt most uncomfortable. Something hurt, a lot. Like something… eating him?

'What on earth is eating me? There is something stinging my legs constantly!'

'Oh, no!' Hanna burst out laughing, a big belly laugh, releasing the tension of her thoughts. 'I forgot that you don't know about our lovely mosquitoes. You are going to feel so itchy, I'm afraid. The mosquitoes, *hyttyset*, come out in the summer evenings. The barbecue has been switched off, so there is no smoke anymore, and nothing to hold them back. Come quickly, let's run back to the cottage and we'll get some 'OFF' – that's a mosquito repellent. It stinks to high heaven but it does the job.'

Hanna and Micheál dashed to the cottage at top speed, Hanna laughing at Micheál's disgusted look. His love for Finland may have been shaken a bit tonight.

Hanna and Micheál were occupying one of the log cabin's upstairs rooms. Hanna had spent many a sleepover there with her teenage girlfriends, and now she had her best friend with her.

Micheál – who was seriously considering becoming the father of her children.

*

Hanna got up early the next morning, having slept very little. There had been a mosquito in the room, but she had felt too tired to get up to kill it – and also unwilling suddenly to disturb her best friend's sleep, as she had been reluctant to face him yet. She had lain awake as the live bait for the squeaky monster, willing it to eat her instead of Micheál.

Micheál was still sleeping when she quietly left the room. The rest of the cottage was also fast asleep, although Hanna's sister's dog Kassu lifted his head and whimpered a little when she came downstairs. She went into the kitchen and drank some water, snatched a *pulla* – a sweet bun – from the cupboard and went outside, bringing Kassu with her.

Kassu was delighted to get out, and ran around the garden happily, sniffing something here, lifting his leg there. Hanna went to sit in the large swing at the back of the cottage. The morning was glorious. The night's dew was still glistening on the early summer growth, and the sun was already high in the sky, warming Hanna nicely. It was only a month to midsummer, when the sun stayed up the longest, almost 24 hours in the south of Finland and the full 24 hours in the north.

Hanna looked around her, enjoying the early summer's peaceful, soul-warming calm. Before her, she could see a new scene in the eye of her imagination: her children running around happily in the cottage garden, playing with their cousin Suvi. She could almost hear their high-pitched laugher and squeals of excitement. A boy and a girl: her children. Silent contentment filled up her heart as she imagined them running around in circles, happy as only the very young can be. In her daydream, it was a hot summer day and the water sprinkler was on, moving from side to side. The children ran away from it, trying not to get wet, but sometimes they ran straight through it just for the excitement of being soaked. She could remember those kinds of days from her own childhood. And she could see her best friend there with her, always by her side, supporting her. Micheál would be her rock, the one who never let her down. The one that would love her, no matter what.

It felt good. It was the happiest picture she had been able to imagine in the many horrible months after Sebastian's betrayal. The shock of having been so wrong about something that had felt so right was slowly starting to fade away. Perhaps she could be happy again. Micheál had come to her rescue when she needed him. He had not given up on her when she had wanted nothing but to sever all ties to Ireland, to forget about it all. He had tracked her down; he had arrived in Helsinki, and had stayed by her side. Micheál was a true friend.

And she could have it all with him. Was it so wrong to want to have children with one's best friend? All the worrying thoughts of the night seemed to fade away in the morning's glory.

Nothing ever seemed so horrible when the sun shone and warmed one to the bone.

She would do it. There would be difficulties to overcome, but that was true for any type of relationship.

## Chapter 14

'*Kengät pois*!'

'How charming,' Micheál muttered to Hanna under his breath. 'This estate agent is really trying hard to sell us this house.'

'Well, *you* are the one who is forever telling me how *true* the Finns are, how honest. And you should know by now that you have to take your shoes off when you walk in the door,' Hanna laughed. Her facial muscles, so underused since her return from Ireland, were back in the game again since Micheál's arrival.

They had spent weeks scouring the newspapers and the internet for houses in Espoo, a leafy town west of Helsinki, which consisted largely of low-density areas of detached houses. Finnish housing estates differed from Irish ones greatly, as all houses were different, built by the purchasers of each site. New was mixed with old, and everything in between. The gardens were always leafy and beautiful.

'I think this is the one!' Micheál said firmly.

'Really – you think so? You've rejected every house we have seen so far.'

'I know, because they were not the right one. But this one is. I love it.'

‘Wow – I didn’t think this was ever going to happen. I liked the last 20 houses but you hated them all with a passion.’

‘I’m sure. Let’s buy it!’ Micheál squealed.

Ten minutes later they had agreed the sale. It was a simple process in Finland: Micheál filled in the written offer form, which formed a contract between the seller and the buyer of all the terms and conditions of the purchase. Once signed by both parties, the sale was good as confirmed. And as soon as Micheál had offered the asking price and accepted all the other conditions the estate agent knew that the seller wanted, the agent asked everyone else who was viewing the house to get out. They would be moving in within two weeks.

Hanna and Micheál had agreed that Micheál would buy the house, while Hanna kept her apartment and rented it out. They didn’t want to complicate their already-complicated future any more than was necessary. Micheál was well off, so it wasn’t difficult for him to purchase the house on his own for cash.

Micheál decided that he would go back to Ireland for a few days, to look in on the business, and to pack and send all the stuff he wanted for his brand new life in Finland. Hanna would focus on getting the apartment packed up and ready for the move to the new house.

Micheál had not given his native land much thought while he had been busy building up his new life in his adopted country. It was good to be home: the view from the Aer Lingus plane window had been very endearing to him, with its patchwork of different shades of greenery, and endless stretches of winding streets of north county Dublin housing estates, constructed during the mad boom of recent years. For a few days, he would understand everything people were saying, and he'd also understand how they were thinking, the silent web of beliefs underlying the interactions between people. He was still too new to Finland to understand even half the stuff that was going on under the bonnet, and at times it got tiresome.

Micheál was more content with his life than he had ever been. His youth had been spent mostly in shame and confusion about his sexuality, although he had escaped the harsh bullying he had seen other gay people exposed to. In his twenties, he had loved building up his business, right after his degree in marketing and event management. Throughout the more difficult early years, he had felt lucky to have such supportive parents, both financially and emotionally. But meeting Hanna had been the best thing yet to happen to him: he felt they were soulmates, and he really loved being around her. She had always accepted him exactly as he was, from the first wonderful moment onward. The months apart from her had been excruciating, and it still gave him cold shivers to think about that time. He couldn't believe that he almost hadn't gone after her.

A few nights later, Micheál was catching up with some business associates in a trendy wine bar in Dublin's city centre when a couple walked in that made him look at them twice. He quickly realised that it was Sofia, with a gorgeous man who had his arm draped around her possessively. Sofia looked good: she radiated happiness, and her well-toned body was showcased by an extremely sexy little outfit. The man looked even better, at least to Micheál's eyes. He was tanned, in the way some people just are no matter what the time of year, and his messy long light-brown hair had the same tanned look as his skin, as if he had spent long hours in the sunshine. *He's obviously not from around here*, Micheál thought. Although Micheál had put his sex life on hold in the past few months, being too focused on other things, this tanned vision reminded him that there were still men out there. Perhaps he would visit *The George* later on, just to see what was on offer in Dublin's gay scene tonight...

Micheál got up to say hello to Sofia and the angelic vision. They were seated by the window, obviously waiting for some more people, as they had asked for a table for four. Micheál sat down at one of the empty chairs.

'Sofia! Great to see you!'

'Micheál!' Sofia's brow cleared when she recalled his name and why she knew him. 'Hanna's friend.'

'That's right. You're looking sensational.'

'Thanks!'

'Remember I was looking for Hanna the last time I saw you? Well, I found her. I went over to Finland straight away after I last saw you.'

'Did you? That's good to hear. How is she?'

'She's good now, although she was really bad when I found her.'

'Oh, how so?'

'She was devastated about Sebastian. Apparently our golden boy was not so golden, but a regular two-timing bastard.'

'What do you mean?'

'Only that he'd got his PA pregnant while carrying on with Hanna at the same time. When Hanna found out, she quite naturally bolted back to Finland ASAP.'

'That certainly explains a lot,' said Sofia. 'I often wondered why she never told me she was leaving or why she never got in touch any more – but then, Finns can be like that at times.'

'Yes, I know all about that now!' chuckled Micheál. 'I've actually been living in Finland these past few months, ever since I went over to see Hanna. I've learned an awful lot about the culture and the language.'

'Have you now? That must have been some shock for you. So, Hanna is over Sebastian now, is she?' Sofia sipped her wine.

'Pretty much – although she's still quiet at times. I've purchased a house in Espoo just now, and she and I are moving in together next week.' Micheál couldn't contain the excitement in his voice. He loved telling everybody about his brave new life.

'You have? Wow – just the two of you?' Micheál could see the puzzlement in Sofia's eyes. Everyone seemed to have such simplistic ideas about relationships. If you were a gay man, you didn't move in with a woman. He understood that it was unorthodox, and he couldn't explain it any more than anyone else, but he was just going with the flow. And the flow felt fabulously good.

'Yes, just the two of us. Platonically, of course. But tell me, now: who is your fabulous friend?' Micheál turned to the vision of perfection sitting beside him, drinking in the essence of this hunk of a man.

'Hi, mate – Aaron Bailey. Great to meet more friends of Sofia's,' Aaron exclaimed in his enthusiastic manner, giving Micheál a knee-weakening grin as he extended his hand. Micheál savoured the touch of his calloused, all-man hand and shivered. Delicious! And Australian on top of everything – just the type he really liked.

'Nice to meet you too. So, you're obviously from down under – what brings you to Ireland?'

'Sofia here. She's some kind of magic woman with the horses. I came over a few months ago to do a course with her – and stayed. We're together now – and we work together. It's bloody brilliant.' Aaron gave Sofia a smouldering look, which was echoed in Sofia's eyes. Micheál could nearly feel the heat emanating from the pair.

'Well done, girl!' Micheál ripped his eyes away from Aaron to congratulate Sofia on her exceptional conquest. 'You've got something special here, haven't you?' he said with a wink.

'I do, don't I?' A big self-satisfactory smile spread across Sofia's face. She looked prettier now, Micheál thought. She had always been a beautiful woman, but there had been a hard edge to her, and she had rarely smiled. She was all smiles now, blooming – but then how could she not be when she had Aaron by her side. Micheál felt a fleeting moment of envy.

'I'd better get back to my colleagues over there, but here's my business card, just in case you want to come over and visit us in Espoo some time.'

'Thanks, we may just do that. I was planning to take Aaron over to Finland while it's still nice over there, before the snow arrives,' Sofia smiled.

‘Yes, the snow is horrible. I’m not looking forward to experiencing my first proper winter in Finland. It was horribly cold when I arrived in April. Ah, the consequences of one’s decisions! But I wouldn’t change a thing about my new life.’

‘Perhaps we’ll see you over there, then?’

‘Let’s hope so,’ Micheál said, throwing one more lingering glance in Aaron’s direction. What a man!

*

Micheál and Hanna spent all of Hanna’s summer holidays getting their new home up and running. The house was in good condition when they bought it, but of course, every surface had to be changed, to reflect their taste. The floors had been laminate wood-effect. Obviously these had to come up immediately – Micheál couldn’t stand anything made of plastic. After hours spent in flooring shops, they decided on solid ash. It was quite an unusual-looking timber, and Micheál loved its light colour the moment he saw it. The walls were all repainted and partially wallpapered in a variety of colours, to express Micheál’s somewhat eclectic but modern taste. Hanna had mostly been willing to go along with his ideas, since she knew that he was good at it: she had seen his creations for weddings and conferences, as well as what he had done with his own apartment in Dublin. Although she was also artistically inclined, her skills had always centred on oral art rather than visual.

Micheál was all in favour of using mostly Finnish design. Naturally, he had incorporated some classic Artek pieces, most of them from Finland's most famous architect-designer Alvar Aalto. He especially loved the lighting range, and had gone a bit mad in the Artek shop in Helsinki. Many a time he thanked his lucky stars that money was no object. Finland was an expensive country – quality never comes cheap.

He was charmed by the tradesmen that had passed through his house during the refurbishment, finding them calm and excellent workers. He marvelled at the way a Finnish plumber would come in, do all the work, and then refuse cash payment, insisting on sending him an invoice – which would include, among other costs, the exact number of kilometres the plumber had travelled to and from Micheál's house and its associated charge. Also, the Finns had got rid of cheques in the nineties, deeming them old-fashioned and impractical, so all invoices were paid by online bank transfer. It was all so civilised!

All was done, finished. Micheál and Hanna were relaxing on the brand new couches that had been delivered earlier in the afternoon. The air still smelled of new paint and new furniture. Hanna felt tired but pleased. She and Micheál would be officially moving in tonight, and they were each to have their own bedroom. Suddenly Hanna realised that she would miss the intimacy of sleeping in the same bed with Micheál. It had been a great comfort to have him there, sleeping by her side, all these months.

Hanna was only just beginning to appreciate fully the huge difference between everyday heterosexual relationships and what she now had with Micheál. "Normal" relationships came with so many unspoken but commonly understood conventions, norms and beliefs, handed down by centuries of social history. She felt so free with Micheál. He would not be jealous of her if she ever found a man she would like to sleep with, and nor would she of him. They were the best of friends, and would always have each other's backs. Hanna felt she could tell Micheál anything. He would not judge her or question her motives. *Perhaps this is what is meant by "unconditional love"*, Hanna thought.

*No expectations*. That was it. And that's what Sebastian had always kept going on about, that "no expectations" was the key to true happiness. She could believe in it now. The thought of Sebastian still made Hanna sad – but she was also able to smile, since she was comfortable with her life now. She had no expectations about her relationship with Micheál. Everything that happened with him felt like a true gift; every moment had an essence of magic in it. She didn't have to pretend to be anything she was not with him. She had even left him, but he had sought her out and wanted to share his life with her.

Micheál was handsome, rich and incredibly sensitive to her needs and wants. He had a great sense of humour – not to mention a great sense of style, as he was always turned out better than most male models were. He had even turned her own wardrobe around, and she loved the new clothes he had insisted on buying her. He had moved to her country and learned her language. He wanted to have babies with her, and had bought them a fine home in a fine area. What more could she possible ever want?

*Well, sometimes a bit of sex would be nice*, Hanna thought, finding herself colouring up a little. But then again, paradoxically, their relationship was pretty good in that regard: there was no sexual tension between them, and she didn't ever feel any kind of physical awkwardness with Micheál. Sexual tension could be fun, Hanna thought, but it hardly ever came without some kind of demand. *It had been perfect with Sebastian*, came fleetingly into Hanna's mind. *Well, apparently it had been "perfect" with others for him, so plenty of baggage there*, she answered herself.

Hanna decided that while she was not renouncing sex entirely, it didn't look to be playing a very important role in her future life. A bit of fun sometimes, perhaps – but that would be all.

Micheál was deliriously happy. As he sipped a glass of wine, he surveyed the results of their efforts to create the perfect home. He had done well. Hanna was a perfect life partner for him. He had had his share of relationships, and had not found much success beyond the first flurry of passion, finding them tiring and full of jealousy. In recent years, he had specialised in one-night stands, when he felt that the urge for physical contact was too much to bear. Despite his own flamboyance, Micheál wasn't fond of high drama in relationships, preferring the quiet type. Yet even his relationships with calmer men seemed to end in primadonna tantrums. And as a moderate drinker – a sensual drinker, he often called it – he could not stand the over-the-top culture of endless rounds at the bar that was so common in Ireland. The Finns sure liked their drink, yet they seemed more reserved.

It felt right settling down with a woman. He chuckled to himself: his mother would be proud. As supportive as she had always been of his sexuality, her little Catholic heart had always secretly hoped that he would "grow out of his gay phase" and settle down with a proper girl. Well, he had surprised himself by doing just that. And he could not wait to hear the proverbial pitter-patter of little feet on his brand-new ash floor.

He adored children, and it had always been one of his biggest regrets not to be able to have them. And then Hanna came along, and from the first moment he had seen her, he had known that there was something very special there. There had not been much time to improvise a meeting in the busy shopping centre in which he had first encountered her, but the gambit of literally bumping into her had worked well, and he had tagged along for long enough to get Hanna's attention – albeit at first, ice-cold attention – and the rest was history. And it all culminated in tonight, when they would officially move in together, into their first home together. Which reminded him – they needed to get going to Hanna's apartment in Munkkivuori, to collect the last bits and pieces.

'Hanna, dear?'

'Yes, Micheál, darling?' It felt nice to speak in English with him. Nowadays, he usually insisted that all their conversations should be conducted in Finnish, and he would only allow himself to speak English when he wanted Hanna to tell him a word's Finnish equivalent. It was astonishing how fast he had picked up the language, but Hanna missed Micheál's sonorous and soft Irish way of speaking English. Finnish was so harsh in comparison, although Micheál with his habitual Midas touch was even able to make it sound good too, much better than the natives.

'Shall we get going? I have a special surprise for you tonight and I don't want us to be late.'

'Oh, what surprise? You have to tell me,' Hanna pleaded with him.

'You're just going to have to wait, Miss Impatient! You'll love it.'

'Huh, well – all right, I'll wait. Let's go.'

Micheál turned away from Hanna, secretly sending a quick text before ushering her into the car.

When Micheál opened the door on their return, Hanna could hear the mournful yet beautiful notes of Baroque violin quartet music in the air – her favourite period of classical music, music made just before the rise of the pianoforte as an instrument. Hanna truly adored the piano, but she would rarely choose to listen to it, as she found it difficult to switch off professionally. To her Finnish melancholic soul, Baroque music spoke loud and clear of the balance of life and death.

Micheál took Hanna's hand and brought her upstairs to her new bedroom. On the bed, there was the most beautiful white evening gown, pure 1950s Hollywood glamour, with a narrow waistline and a big bell skirt. And on the table was a bright red lipstick to finish off the look.

Micheál withdrew from her room, hearing her surprised exclamations, and went to change into something more suitable for the evening. He returned a few minutes later wearing a three-piece suit, leaving the jacket behind since it was a warm night. He had slicked his hair back with some sort of oil, and he looked delicious.

'You look stunning, Hanna. I've been dreaming about seeing you in a Marilyn dress like this for a long time.'

'Oh, Micheál, I don't know what to say. It is beautiful. I feel like I'm suddenly on a Hollywood set, getting ready for filming.'

‘Well, my darling, perhaps you are,’ Micheál said in his best Hollywood accent, and he escorted the laughing girl on his arm downstairs and out onto the terrace in the back garden, where well-dressed caterers – handsome young men, of course; anything Micheál did was always aesthetically pleasing – were busily attending to a barbecue feast. Although the evening was still fairly bright (the Finnish summer evenings never get properly dark), the caterers had hung up some attractive colourful lanterns with candles. The coal barbecue was still in full flame, and the round table was laid out for two, with a long white tablecloth and candles.

‘Oh, Micheál – it is beautiful. And you did this just for the two of us, just for me?’

‘Yes, anything for my special girl.’ Micheál helped Hanna to sit down. ‘I am so glad to be starting my new life with you in this gorgeous house, in this most amazing country.’

‘Me too. I’m so glad you came over. I was so unhappy after... well, after I left Ireland.’

‘I was dreadfully unhappy, too. I have never missed anyone as much as I missed you. I couldn’t bear it in the end – I just had to come after you! You know I love you so much, my darling, don’t you?’

‘I do know it. And I love you, too.’

*

Hanna opened her eyes. Then she remembered where she was: in her new home with Micheál. Her mouth settled into a big smile. I must be the luckiest girl alive, she thought to herself, stretching out in the bed, cat-like. The brand new satin bed sheets felt so comfortable, enveloping her in another manifestation of Micheál's love for her, for their life together.

Hanna could hear Micheál rustling away in the kitchen: probably making them breakfast. Hanna sighed again with deep pleasure. *Where would I be now if everything had worked out with Sebastian?* The thought came unbidden into Hanna's mind. Her brow furrowed. She didn't want to think about *him* ever again. He had hurt her so badly.

*But had he?*

Suddenly, out of nowhere, images of another happy morning, in another lifetime, popped into her mind. Sebastian, not Micheál, in the kitchen, preparing breakfast. They had been so good together. So really, how had it all ended so badly?

Ambushed unexpectedly by the pain that had so recently been receding, Hanna curled up in a foetal position. She missed Sebastian.

*But he's a bastard, a two-timing coward.*

Yet Hanna could feel that what had once been such a tight knot in her stomach didn't feel so tight anymore. Perhaps she had been too hard on the man. She had never given him an opportunity to explain himself; she had simply run, in shock, back to Finland, when Cathy had dropped the bomb on her doorstep about her and Sebastian's baby. Hanna was happy now, with Micheál, so happy that it was difficult to maintain the same level of anger and shock. After all, as Sebastian had explained to her, her emotions were only a reflection of her own beliefs.

And what had she believed at the time? That she had got it all wrong. That Sebastian had lied to her by insinuating love for her, since he was capable of doing all that other stuff behind her back. She had believed, like most other people apparently believe, that if you are in a relationship with someone, it is an exclusive sexual arrangement. That when you really care about someone – even if it is early days for the relationship – that it implied marriage and children, down the line. They had sometimes talked about children's names, in a general way. Hanna had liked the name Amelia for a girl, and Sebastian Toby for a boy. But nothing beyond that had been discussed about children and marriage.

They hadn't talked either about what would happen once Hanna finished her contract in Ireland and the time came to make some actual decisions about their relationship. There hadn't been any reason to do so, as they had thought they would have many more months together in Ireland before D-day – or F-Day, for Finland.

Hanna could now admit to herself that perhaps she had been a bit hasty in her retreat back to Finland. But she hadn't felt able to deal with the shocking discovery of Cathy's growing belly at the time, and the only thing that had made any sense to her was to abandon ship – or island – as fast as possible.

Months later, Hanna wondered about that decision for the first time. She pulled the bedcovers over her head and closed her eyes tightly, the tears still bursting out of them. What if she had got it wrong, somehow? What if there was a logical explanation to it all? But then again – what could it be? That Sebastian somehow accidentally got that woman pregnant? How likely was that?

Forgiveness. But to forgive what? That Hanna herself had expected exclusivity when they had not made any contract – written or verbal – to that effect? That Sebastian had different moral expectations than her? That she had imagined it all? But Hanna had not imagined Sebastian's love, she was sure of that. Being loved by Micheál had given her self-confidence a boost and she could now recognise the feeling of being loved. Sebastian *had* loved her – he had just never said so. Perhaps, for such an advanced being as he, the concept of sexual exclusivity was outdated. Was it necessary anyway, for a happy relationship?

Look at Micheál, for example. Hanna would not be upset if she found out that he was sleeping with other men. Perhaps she would find it a bit annoying if he was bringing them over to their home together all the time, creating noise and hassle for Hanna, but that was still different. So why the different rules for the different types of relationships? Micheál could sleep around, as far as Hanna was concerned, but Sebastian could not?

Hanna sighed heavily. Relationships could be so much hard work. She pulled the bedcovers away. She just couldn't be unhappy on this first morning of her new life with Micheál. Anyhow, the smell of coffee alone could always bring a smile to a Finn's face!

## *Chapter 15*

*Today is the day*, Tim thought nervously. Today he was going to ask Cathy out on a date. It had been some weeks now since his gig, and he had not been able to work up the courage to approach her. True, he had been out of the country touring, and hadn't been to Sebastian's office since the gig. But these were just excuses, he knew. He had chickened out.

Not today.

He knew Cathy would be in the office as he had checked it with Sebastian; he also knew that Sebastian wouldn't be. He would just walk up there and somehow manage to get the words out to ask her to join him for lunch. How hard could it be? Very hard, it seemed.

Tim used his own key to let himself into the office. His palms were wet and his knees were shaking. He was a wreck. He could not remember ever being this nervous in his life. He walked up to the door of Cathy's office and knocked. Receiving no answer, he pushed the door ajar. Cathy was doing something at the photocopier, her back to the door. She looked so pretty. She was wearing a pencil skirt, very official and proper, with court shoes, but the overall look was softened by the pink cardigan she was wearing. Her blonde hair was down and some tendrils had escaped from behind her ears. She turned around and jumped.

'Tim! You scared me! I thought you were Sebastian.'

'Sorry! I didn't mean to give you a shock.' Tim felt embarrassed. Already this was not going well. He could feel the colour creeping up his neck. He tried to give Cathy an apologetic smile, but he was not sure what it looked like. Probably like a monkey in a torture chamber.

'You've been away a lot, haven't you?'

'Yes, I've been gigging abroad a bit...'

'It's going well for you, then, your music? I enjoyed the night Sebastian and I came to listen to you. You were very good.'

'Thanks, Cathy,' Tim grinned. She had liked it. She looked adorable just standing there. And she was actually having a conversation with him. She had never done that before. It felt fabulously good, to be talking to her. He could stay forever.

'Um, did you want something, Tim?' Cathy asked kindly.

'Sorry.' *I have to stop saying that*. 'I was wondering... if you'd like, uh, I mean...if you haven't eaten yet... like, lunch, with me, like, now...' *Brilliant. That was pathetic*.

'I'd love to.'

'You would? Are you sure?'

Cathy started to laugh. The look of disbelief on Tim's face was so funny. The boy couldn't hide his emotions at all. Which was quite lovely, in fact. And he looked sort of... handsome, if one could apply that word to him. Definitely nice. He made her smile and that had to be a good thing.

'Yes, I'm sure. I'm just finishing up here now. Would you like to wait a few minutes for me to get ready, and we can go then?'

'Um, sure, that's great. Sorry – I mean, fantastic! I'll wait out here, yeah?'

'Yes, that would be fine. I'll see you in a minute.'

'Great! Grand! I'll be just out here, waiting!'

Cathy smiled to herself as he left the office. She had always thought Tim puppy-like, which used to irritate her, but somehow she was now finding that same characteristic quite endearing. She felt light, almost giddy, as if she were about to giggle. She decided to go with it. Cathy had never before giggled in her life.

They went to Milano's. Cathy thought back to the last time she had been there, believing she was on a date with Sebastian. This time, it actually felt like a date. Tim made such a fuss of her, taking her coat, escorting her to the table and pulling her chair out for her. He chatted to her nervously the entire time, asking her about a hundred times if she was okay and whether everything was fine. She had never been fussed over so much in her life. A first for her – and she was enjoying the attention. Normally she felt uncomfortable on a first date, hating the awkwardness of it all –

not that she had been on a proper date for a long time, having spent so many years daydreaming about Sebastian. She could only shake her head in wonderment: what had she been thinking?

'You are okay now, aren't you?' Tim asked, his voice full of concern, and the colour heightened on his cheeks.

Cathy giggled some more. She could get used to this giggling business, she thought. She felt so girly. So looked after. And yet so in control. 'You are so funny, Tim. Do stop fussing, please – I'm fine. Just relax.'

'Oh, I'm sorry – I just want to make sure you're having a good time.'

'I am, please believe me – you're doing a great job.' Cathy was rewarded with a huge grin. Tim sure knew how to smile. And Cathy had never actually realised how well he looked when he smiled. *Time to put the boy at ease*, she thought.

'You played so well that night when I and Sebastian came to see you. And you looked so happy. How does it feel to play?'

Tim visibly relaxed. This he could talk about all day. 'I feel so good when I play. Traditional Irish music is so joyful, and there's nothing in this world that I enjoy doing more than playing my guitar.'

'It shows. You looked... blissful. I don't know if I've ever been that happy in my life. I think I envy you a little.'

'You, envy *me*? But you are so amazing, so talented and...' Tim blushed at his outburst. He had revealed a lot more than he had intended. He was so worried that Cathy wasn't going to like him, when there was nothing he wanted more in this world. There was just something about the girl that drew him in, always had. From the first moment he had seen her, he had wanted to get to know her. She was so... sophisticated and ladylike. She was always so perfectly turned out, and she held herself so well.

'Oh, Tim, you make me blush with all your compliments. But honestly, I do envy you your... how would I say it... your carefree manner. It's as if it is all just so easy for you.'

'Well, then – we both envy each other,' said Tim. 'I've always envied you your elegance. You are just so perfect, in every way...'

They were both blushing now. Luckily, the waitress came over to take their orders, and they had a minute to cool down. Cathy was enjoying herself. Tim was so funny. How had she not realised before now that he could be such wonderful company, and so much fun? Well – if she was honest with herself, she knew that she had not been in the right frame of mind before now, to find someone... so nice. She had always looked for the wrong type of person, and therefore had always found the wrong type. *Be careful what you wish for*, is what Sebastian would have said to her now, if he had been here. *Will that man ever leave my mind?* She sighed, smiling. She did care for Sebastian, but finally she had understood that she didn't love him.

But talking of love – she was falling, fast. It felt so good to smile, really smile properly – not the usual polite, businesslike expression she usually wore. A real grin that felt like a caress on her face. She could feel her heart beating fast. She was full of life, alive, and very present in her "now". At last she could understand what Sebastian was always going on about. Previously, she had barely scratched the surface of the knowledge Sebastian shared with his audiences. Now she could feel it, inside her, her whole being alive with it.

'Tim, I want to thank you for asking me out today. I'm having such a wonderful time with you.'

'You're welcome, Cathy – any time. I was actually wondering if you'd like to go out with me again soon?'

'I most certainly would like that. I'm free this Saturday – would that suit you?'

'I'll make it suit! What time?' Tim looked as if he was bursting out of his skin.

'How about midday?'

'Cool. Leave it with me and I'll think of something fun for us to do. Can I take your mobile number?'

‘Of course you can. And I like the sound of “doing something fun” together. I’m beginning to see what Sebastian is always saying about the purpose of life being to have fun. I’m very new to the whole concept – so you may have to bear with me while I find my sea legs.’

‘“Fun” is my middle name,’ Tim announced proudly.

‘I believe you. You are the happiest person I know; I love that about you.’

*Love…? She likes me*! Tim’s brain screamed joyfully.

*

Cathy had made up her mind. She was going to tell Sebastian what she had said to Hanna. It was time to stop worrying about her job. If Sebastian wanted to fire her, so be it. She couldn’t bear feeling such guilt anymore. She was so happy with Tim; the thought of having destroyed someone else’s chance for happiness – and Sebastian’s at that – weighed too heavily on her mind.

‘Sebastian, would you have a minute to talk to me?’ Cathy said to him at the door of his office, her voice wobbling slightly. She was more nervous than she had ever been in her life. This was the hardest thing she had ever had to do, but she knew it was right. Sebastian deserved to know the truth.

'Sure, Cathy – can you just give me a minute to finish up here? Why don't you go back into your office and I'll come over in a minute,' Sebastian said cheerfully.

'Okay. I'll wait for you.' Cathy went back to her room and sat down heavily. She felt slightly nauseous. This was going to be awful, for both of them. Why had she done what she had done? It had made perfect sense at the time, but now it made none. She felt an urge to pray that Sebastian would be able to forgive her, someday – and she wasn't even religious.

'Sorry, Cathy, I was just finishing up some good stuff. The energy is flowing again so well, and my writing is great at the moment.'

*Oh no – he is feeling so good, and I'm going to rip it all apart.*

'Sebastian, why don't you sit down, please? There is something I have to tell you. I did something horrible, something that you are not going to like.'

'Oh, I can't imagine you ever doing anything wrong!' Sebastian was still feeling great, and wasn't picking up on Cathy's serious mood. She had probably got an order wrong, or something.

'Sebastian, please listen to me. It's about Hanna.'

She had Sebastian's attention now. His face blanched. He looked shocked.

‘I said something horrible to her before she went back to Finland.’

‘I didn’t know you had talked to her before she went,’ Sebastian said in a small voice.

‘I called over to her house.’

‘How did you know where she lived?’

‘It’s a long story. Or perhaps I should tell you from the beginning.’

‘Go on.’

‘Remember when I convinced you to hire me as your personal assistant, years ago?’

‘Yes...’ Sebastian didn’t know where this was going.

‘I thought I was in love with you. I thought that I could make you love me if you could just see how good I was at my job, how compatible we would be, if I only tried hard enough.’

‘Is this something to do with what you asked me at Tim’s gig?’

‘Yes and no. Yes, in terms of me realising that I had been wrong all along, that you were never going to love me. That I didn’t actually love you... you know, properly, with passion. Like the way I love Tim.’

Sebastian smiled at this. He was so pleased that Tim and Cathy had got together. The old saying about "opposites attracting" must have something to it. But his smile faltered, as he remembered that Cathy had said something to Hanna.

'What did you say to Hanna?'

'Oh, Sebastian, I've done something so horrible!' Cathy was starting to weep. This was such a dreadful situation. She was going to break his heart all over again, just when he was starting to get his life back together. 'I lied to her... about us. I... I told her that... I was pregnant and... and that you were the father.' Cathy was crying now in earnest.

'You said what...?' Sebastian couldn't believe his ears. He got up abruptly, and walked back into his office in a daze. He felt empty. Suddenly, Hanna's bizarre reaction made sense. The disgust in her voice, the last time they had talked: she had believed he had slept with Cathy.

*How could Cathy have done this?* Sebastian was stunned by her malice. What kind of person would do something like that? A desperate one. Sebastian had never given Cathy the slightest hint he cared for her, yet it was obvious that Cathy had believed he'd change his mind. Unbelievable. Had she done something like this before? Probably. But then, it didn't matter, as he had never been serious about anyone else before Hanna. And it hurt. Cathy's plotting had torn away his love. Hanna was gone. And it had all been a lie.

But then... then maybe he still had a chance with her! All he had to do was to tell Hanna that Cathy had lied, that none of it was true.

Racing home, Sebastian packed his bag with random clothes, phoned for a taxi, and got to Dublin airport in record time, having promised the taxi driver a hefty tip. With astonishing luck, he found an airline willing to sell him a ticket to Finland on a flight leaving within the hour. Now he just had to get on the plane. But it wasn't happening, not fast enough for his liking. Sebastian waited impatiently for the boarding call to be announced.

His plan was simple: he was going to stalk Hanna outside the Helsinki concert hall and tell her everything. He trusted that he would figure out the details once he got there.

*

Hanna had had a great day at work; everything had been effortless. She loved working in the new *Musiikkitalo* – literally, "music house", the new concert hall in Helsinki. The building was ultra-modern, the facilities were great and they had bought a brand new Steinway concert grand piano. She was over the moon working on the glorious instrument. The old concert grand had been good – and she would still be working on it, as it was used in one of the smaller auditoriums – but it didn't compare to the new one. Her new Steinway had the most beautiful sound. Each piano was unique, made out of natural materials, and every piano sounded different. Her new baby clearly contained timber from a magic forest; it was so melodic, in particular, in the mid-treble, which was almost impossible to change, if the sound wasn't naturally there. She had spent the last week preparing it, working endlessly at all aspects of the mechanics, regulating the action and toning the hammers like a mad woman, as well as making sure the tuning held after her pitch move, needing multiple adjustments to set the strings in their new, stretched position. It was now perfect for the very special concert it was to be used for tonight.

Hanna had started playing the piano again since Micheál had arrived back in her life. Today, she had spent the last hour of her workday playing her perfect instrument, enjoying the experience, in the guise of finding any last kinks to be corrected in the voicing. There were none. Her soft pedal toning work was immaculate, too. But since there was nobody there who could question her methods, she had enjoyed her own private concert. Her body, mind and soul were still vibrating with pleasure from the glorious music she had let flow through her, and the melodies were still playing in her head.

Hanna left the concert hall via the main entrance on Mannerheimintie. The weather was still glorious; the sun was shining, adding to her mood. Autumn was just around the corner, but there was no sign of it just yet. Hanna was busy hatching a plan to take Micheál for a swim in one of the great lakes in Espoo, when she heard her name being called. She turned around to see who was shouting for her in such an obviously foreign accent.

Hanna was not prepared for what she saw.

*Sebastian.*

Her heart stopped. And broke again. All the pain came flooding back. Hanna turned around and began running as panic engulfed her. She couldn't cope with the pain for a second time; she had to get away, as fast as possible.

Sebastian saw the look of fright on Hanna's face before she turned and sprinted away from him. He had a terrible feeling of déjà vu. She was leaving him again. But he had to explain the big misunderstanding, to make her realise that Cathy had lied, had only told her those things out of jealousy. He had to have a chance to make it all right again. There was only one thing for him to do: sprint after her.

'Hanna, Hanna, please stop! There is something important I need to tell you!' Sebastian pleaded as he began to catch up with Hanna. He didn't want to crowd her. Although he could have easily overtaken her, he hoped she would decide to stop. He could see other people on the street giving them strange looks, and he hoped that nobody called the police. He wasn't a stalker!

'Hanna, please. Just hear me out this once! And then I'll leave you alone.'

Hanna could feel her strength weakening. She wasn't super-fit, had never been a fast runner, and she knew from their time together in Ireland that Sebastian should have caught up with her by now. The fact that he hadn't meant that he was holding back. She decided to stop. She didn't have much choice, anyhow, as she wouldn't have been able to run much further.

She saw a vacant park bench at Töölönlahti and headed towards it. She ran through the small park to sit by the sea. She was panting so hard that it would take her a few minutes to catch her breath. Her heart raced erratically. Most of its missed beats were not caused by the run, but by the sudden appearance of Sebastian.

She had loved him so much. And then she had been hurt so much by what he had done. She had worked hard to recreate some sort of life for herself. And yet here she was again, the familiar pain overwhelming her, the strength of it taking her by surprise. What was Sebastian doing in Helsinki? She had believed herself safe, in a different country, far away from Dublin. And why now? She had been afraid of him showing up unexpectedly during the first month or two after her return, but since it had never happened, she had gradually come to put that particular fear aside.

Sebastian approached the bench slowly, giving Hanna time to think. She was facing away from him, her back rigid, and her shoulders heaving with the effort of her escape. Yet she had stopped for him, had sought out a quiet park bench, seemingly ready to hear him out. Sebastian could feel his heart leaping for joy. It was wonderful to see her again. It had been too long, and he had missed her so much.

'Hanna. Thank you for stopping for me,' Sebastian called from a few meters away, not wanting to startle Hanna. She had yet to turn around to see him, her emotional and physical turmoil very evident from the set of her shoulders.

'I'm so glad to see you again. I've missed you.' Sebastian approached the bench and sat down at the far end, carefully. 'I was so sad for so long when you left me. I was confused – I didn't understand what I had done wrong. I felt the last time we spoke, you had decided that I had done something wrong. You told me, in no uncertain terms, to leave you alone. I have done so. But the reason I'm here now is that Cathy has just told me something that she said to you before you left Ireland. Something that *isn't true*.'

Hanna turned to look at Sebastian. Could it be right? Had Cathy lied? She wouldn't trust him so easily.

'Cathy told me that she had said to you that she was pregnant, and that the child was mine. Is this what she told you, Hanna?'

Hanna looked at Sebastian, her emotions in turmoil. She nodded her head slightly.

'Oh, Hanna. It is not true! She was just jealous of our relationship. For some crazy reason, Cathy thought she could make me love her if you went away. Hanna: I love *you*, not her or anyone else. I will only love you. Please, Hanna, I need to have you back in my life.'

Hanna just sat there, looking at Sebastian. She was in shock. She didn't know what to think, what to believe. It all sounded so... strange. Why would Cathy do such a thing? It didn't make sense. She shook her head. How could someone be so cruel?

Hanna wanted to believe Sebastian. She had loved him so much, and it broke her heart again to hear him say that he loved her. She had longed to hear those words, but had been afraid to ask him outright, to burst their lovely bubble. She had wanted to say it to him so many times, had said it in so many other ways: in gestures, in her smiles, in her kisses. Desperately, she willed the walls of her pretty new life to hold up.

And it was all Sebastian's fault. He had come back, trying to destroy her again. Anger flared up inside her. It was not fair. She had dealt with the pain caused by him, she had put him into a box never to be opened again, and here he was again, torturing her.

‘I don’t care. I have a new life now, and I’m not interested in your lies, or anyone else’s lies. I have moved on. Don’t bother me any more.’ Hanna got up and walked away.

Sebastian was stunned. He had been sure that once Hanna heard what he had to say, she would fall into his arms and they would live happily ever after. He had been so elated from the moment he had heard Cathy tell him the real reason why Hanna had left him. He had believed that they could now go back to normal, back to their life together, continue from where they left off. He had missed her so much. Their shared time in Ireland had been so perfect. It couldn’t just end like this. But here she was walking away from him. Again. Why was he always seeing just her back, moving away from him? It was a nightmare that kept on repeating itself, over and over again.

Hanna’s tears flowed freely down her cheeks. She walked blindly away from Sebastian, without paying much attention to where she was going. It all hurt like hell. The familiar pain of the months after Ireland had returned. She wanted to turn around, to go back to Sebastian, to feel his love again, but somehow she walked on, every step heavier than the last.

## Chapter 16

Much later – perhaps an hour or two later, Hanna wasn't sure – she took in her surroundings. She had walked home to Munkkivuori. Her feet ached, but she welcomed the physical pain. It was easier to bear than the anguish she felt inside. Her tears had dried on her face. She could taste the salt when she licked her dry lips.

Hanna sat down on a bench in the forest. Through the trees, she could see her building. She had missed her forests when she was in Ireland. They felt so safe, the dark green of the evergreens enveloping her like a comfort blanket. She loved the smell of the trees and the pine needles on the ground. There were only a few single people about, walking their dogs. The land of the lonely. They didn't pay her any attention, averting their eyes from her quickly if they accidentally looked in her direction. She really appreciated that just now. She needed to be alone.

The storm in her head had quietened down. The physical exhaustion from the long walk had zapped her energy and calmed her down mentally. Hanna felt so tired, but she didn't want to move. It was so soothing in the forest and she simply sat there, being, not doing.

But there was to be no peace. Her phone started ringing. It had rung a few times during her walk but it had been easy to ignore then. Hanna got a fright when the loud tone started its usual banging. She'd have to change it again – this sound would forever bear negative associations with the ruined moment. She felt her heart beating anxiously, believing that Sebastian had tracked her down. She was afraid to look at her phone, but eventually pulled it out of her handbag. It was Micheál, her guardian angel. Always there for her in her hour of need.

'Micheál. I'm all right,' said Hanna, anticipating Micheál's frantic query.

'Hanna, where are you? I've been so worried. Why haven't you answered your phone? I've called so many times, left you messages. What is happening?' Micheál sounded panicked.

'Sebastian showed up.'

'What, where, when? I can't believe it! Hanna, tell me everything.'

'He was waiting for me outside the *Musiikkitalo*.'

'Oh my God – did you talk to him? What did he say?'

'He said... he said...' Hanna began sobbing again.

'Hanna, where are you? Tell me and I'll come and collect you straight away.'

'I'm... in the forest... behind my apartment block in Munkkivuori.'

'Don't go anywhere. I'll be there in a jiffy.'

'Okay.'

Hanna felt a little better. Everything hurt. But Micheál was on his way.

Within minutes, Hanna heard hurried footsteps, and smiled. She would have known Micheál's steps anywhere. Only he could strut like he was on a runway while hurrying to rescue a friend.

'Hanna, darling, there you are.' Micheál wrapped Hanna in his arms. 'Why didn't you come straight home to me? I would have looked after you, you know that.'

'I don't know, I couldn't think. I just walked blindly, and then I was here.'

'Darling, what happened? Did Sebastian really show up?'

'Yes, he did. First I panicked and ran, but you know, he used to be a sprinter – I couldn't possibly outrun him.'

'Oh, Hanna. Only you would run in that situation! But then what happened? Did you talk to him?'

'He talked to me. He said... he said that Cathy had lied about the baby. But I can't believe that! Why would anyone do something like that? It can't be true.'

'Cathy lied? But that makes so much sense. I never really believed Sebastian was a two-timing bastard, he just didn't seem the type.'

'It makes sense to you? Really? But why would Cathy do something like that?'

'I forget about you honest Finns. Obviously, she loved Sebastian, and thought that she could get him if you were out of the picture. But how did Sebastian find out?'

'Cathy told him.'

'Wow – first lie, and then tell – why on earth?'

'Something about her changing her mind. But – could it really be true? That he never... you know... was with her?'

'Of course. Sebastian seemed to be so in love with you at the time. It didn't make sense for him to be going behind your back.'

'He said he loved me. He's never said that before.'

'The boy loves you – happy days! But... what did you say to him?'

'Oh, that I didn't believe him. And that I had moved on. Which I have! I have just got my life back together again. I can't have anybody messing that up.'

'But Hanna – he loves you.'

'Yes, but what about us, and our great life together? I can't just leave you now. You moved to Finland for me.'

'Hanna. I love you, you know that. But I can't give you everything a man should. I know you love me, but you love Sebastian, too. You were totally broken up when I first got here, all because of him.'

'I know that – but what if he hurts me again?'

'Hanna,' said Micheál gently, '*He* didn't hurt you the first time.'

'Oh.' Hanna's mind was reeling. Maybe Micheál was right. Everything was coming apart. She had been so sure of how bad a person Sebastian was, but now it looked like nothing had actually happened. She felt duped. She had suffered so much. And why?

'That bitch! I'm going to kill her!'

'Now, there is my Hanna! You're coming back to us,' Micheál laughed, giving Hanna a squeeze. She was still curled up under his protective arm. She had sat up rigidly to proclaim her murderous intent, but sank back into Micheál's embrace, feeling some of the tension dissipate with her outburst. Hanna was starting to feel stupid. Cathy's lies had caused her entire life to be taken apart, and for no reason.

It was all so clear to her now. She had never believed that Sebastian would stay with her. He had been too good to be true. The famous Sebastian O'Reilly, interested in Hanna? Sebastian, who was so good at everything, so brilliant and intelligent. It had been so flattering to have him pay attention to her. It had felt amazing: like being a princess to Ireland's celebrity prince. But she wasn't a real princess – her royal career had ended in tears. An impostor, a wannabe.

And hadn't he helped to keep her down, by never telling her that he loved her? She realised now that she had felt insecure with him, even though he had made her very happy. She had been on a high with him in Ireland, but had always deep down felt that high to be artificial, something that wouldn't last. And so she had been easily convinced by Cathy that Sebastian didn't love her.

*It was all in my own head*, Hanna thought, sighing heavily. *I believed I wasn't good enough for him, and I was proven right when Cathy came to me with her lies.*

She hadn't realised it before. She had truly believed that she was not good enough for him. That he could never really be seriously interested in her, as she was nothing special.

A startling discovery.

Hanna felt her head expanding. Information flooded in. This explained a lot of things about her previous relationships. She had never been comfortable with anyone, leaving them all before they had a chance to leave her. Now she understood that she had done this to herself. She had destroyed her relationships rather than risk being shown to be not good enough. And she had left Sebastian, too.

Sebastian had always told her that we create our own reality. Her reality had proven to her that she wasn't good enough for him, and had given her a way out of the relationship before he had the opportunity to leave her. As he always said, she had been fully motivated either towards pleasure or away from pain – in this case, 100% motivated away from the pain of Sebastian leaving her.

*But I am good enough. I don't need to try to be anything that I am not. I'm fine just as I am. He came after me.*

Hanna felt a new calm inside her. Her lack of belief in herself had been tied up in anxieties about her looks, her talents, her charms – but she could see now that it had all been groundless, a group of beliefs that no longer had any hold over her. She was special. None of it mattered. He loved her. Contrasting how she had felt with Sebastian in Ireland with how she always felt around Micheál also helped her to get a new perspective. She had always felt good enough for Micheál's love. Clearly, she had a lot of hang-ups about what a "real" relationship was, and had come to believe that she could not live up to those standards. She hadn't been able to bear the pressure of waiting for Sebastian to go off and cheat on her – and when it had "happened", she had fled.

But her relationship with Micheál had been free from all of her own prejudices. Micheál couldn't cheat on her, as there was nothing to cheat. And perhaps it ought to be the same way with Sebastian. He had told her that he loved her, and wanted to be with her: was that not all she needed? Hanna had always felt free to love Micheál and to be good enough to receive his love. And perhaps she could feel so with Sebastian. Her darling Micheál, always helping her out, even in self-discovery. Fine-tuning, indeed.

Sebastian had often explained that once you discover a negative belief, it will appear illogical, and the hold it has on you will loosen, as it is revealed for what it is: something that doesn't belong in your system. Hanna could feel this deep in her gut. A tight knot that had always been there was now released, gone. She felt peaceful. She felt good enough.

*I love Sebastian*, Hanna admitted to herself. It didn't cause an anxiety attack any more. *And he loves me. And he is here in Finland! Just amazing...*

'Let's go home, Micheál. And plan how I can get that man back into my life.'

'Wonderful, Hanna – that's what I like to hear. You two were always so good together. I'll make you some dinner when we get home, and we can start planning,' Micheál said. He couldn't take it when Hanna was unhappy; it cut him deeply, and made him miserable too. He didn't care what the consequences of Hanna's plans would be to him, as long as his darling was happy again. He had enjoyed his time with her in Finland, and if it was coming to an end, then so be it. He felt a fleeting stab of pain: one day, he'd hoped to have children with Hanna. But he'd be fine; he'd always been fine, except when he didn't have Hanna in his life.

Micheál had noticed that Hanna had still been sad when she was on her own, when she believed that nobody was looking. There had been a veil of melancholy hanging over her ever since he had come to Finland to rescue her, and he had been disappointed to see that no matter what he did, that veil refused to lift completely. Until tonight. Micheál could see that a big change had happened inside her. That boy Sebastian seemed to have some ingredient that agreed with Hanna so well that she couldn't survive without getting her fill of it on a regular basis. The solution was simple: reintroduce Sebastian into her diet. Micheál would do everything in his power to make that a reality.

*

Sebastian sat on his hotel bed, aimlessly flicking through the TV channels. Hanna had rejected him, again. She had said that she had moved on. But he had been so sure of her love when she was in Ireland. They had been so good together. The romance had bloomed easily and passionately, and Sebastian had been more smitten that ever before. And Hanna hadn't been able to get enough of him. She had jumped into the relationship willingly and passionately, all doors open and in an entirely uninhibited manner

– and had also exited it with almost as much intensity. It made his head spin to even think about it. The girl was a tornado. Yet, she fascinated him.

Thinking about it now, he hadn't always been able to tell if Hanna was enjoying herself or not, even when she had verbally assured him that she was. The cultural differences between the Irish and the Finns seemed small, yet every now and again he had been at a total loss with her. He understood that in principle, cultural beliefs, like any other beliefs, were just thoughts that groups of people had produced so often that it seemed impossible that there could be an alternative. That's why he had always enjoyed travelling so much. He had been able to tidy up a lot of his own ingrained beliefs by realising that there were many ways to think about certain matters that he had never been able to see.

Yet this theory had not helped him when Hanna had got annoyed with him. For example, when he had kept asking her if she was okay all the time in the first few weeks. He'd had to learn the hard way: she had gone crazy when he had asked her one time too often, and had explained to him that it was tiring to have to stop whatever she was doing, every time he asked, to consider whether she was, in fact, okay. Sebastian learned that it was something Finns never asked each other, which meant that they took it absolutely literally as a serious question. It was similar to the Irish casual use of "How are you?", which Hanna had told him used to drive her potty – until she realised that she didn't have to think about it but just say, “I’m fine”. So was this one of those moments again, where he had totally misread the cultural signals? Or did Hanna actually mean that she didn’t love him? It was exhausting.

He wasn’t giving up so easily this time, regardless of the emotional whiplash. There was a connection at a deeper level between them, and he was willing to bet that it went well beyond the bounds of any cultural differences. He would pursue her until he was absolutely, 100% sure that she did not want to see him ever again. Only then would he leave her alone for good. Unless of course she changed her mind and decided that she loved him instead. The possibility brought a smile to his face, and he decided to call it a night. After all, he had at least been able to see her again. No point worrying about any of it now, he thought; if she truly didn’t want him, he’d have worried about it all twice. He said his mantra, did a couple of deep breathing exercises and went to sleep, peacefully.

*

Hanna was nervous. And excited.

It had been pretty impossible to focus on her work that day, but she had got through it. Realising that any sort of fine work requiring total focus was out of the question, she had settled down to some cleaning instead. She vacuumed out all her pianos, using a big paint brush to get the dust off the precious metal frames. She polished all the brass, and gave the polyester finish a fine buffing with her cloth. Her instruments shone beautifully, but her mind was still a whirlwind of emotions.

Hanna couldn't wait to see Sebastian again. She hoped he had not been discouraged yesterday by her "leave me alone, I never want to see you again" routine. Surely he'd come back again today, just to see if she had actually meant it? He had flown all the way to Helsinki – he'd hardly give up after one go, would he? Today she would tell him – if she was to have the chance – that she loved him. Which in itself was the biggest, most nervewracking moment of her life: Hanna had lived for 30 years, and had never declared her love to anyone, apart from her darling Micheál. She didn't think she had even said it to her parents or her sister. The words were sacred, like a spell that was not to be used in vain.

In English-speaking countries, "I love you" seemed to be carelessly bandied about a great deal. But then again, the words themselves were easy, slipping effortlessly off the tongue. The letter combination of "l-o" in "love" just begged to be projected out, with puckered lips. The Finnish equivalent, meanwhile – *rakastan sinua* – came from deep within, with the rolling "r" to begin with, followed by all the back vowels, the "a" pronounced deep in the throat. Very heavy stuff, and not to be thrown around without extreme care.

Four o'clock. Finally, it was time to go. Hanna shook with the effort of keeping her emotions at bay, getting herself out of the front door in one piece without fainting. He'd better be there, after her mental suffering all day. She approached the large glass doors of the main entrance. *Is he there? Is he there?* ran through her mind on a continuous loop. She opened the first of the double doors. *He is*! Hanna could see Sebastian, standing further back from the main doors. He looked serious. Hanna smiled: a big smile that pulled her cheeks further and further back. Her smile held all the pressure she had felt since yesterday, and it was almost painful. Her heartbeat was insanely fast, and her legs carried her through the doors of their own accord.

Sebastian turned to see Hanna coming down the steps. She was smiling widely, and his heart nearly stopped with relief. She was coming towards him, fast, and he opened his arms for her. Hanna slammed into him so hard that they nearly fell over. His hug was tight, her arms around his neck even tighter. They stayed like that for a long while. Time had stopped. The moment of their embrace was an eternity, with no beginning and no end, no need for the future or the past. It contained everything.

The desire for life grew, and for all the wonderful experiences that it would provide. The sense of self returned, and with it, understanding of their separate natures. Each pulled back, just enough to be able to see each other's faces. Hanna drank in the sight of him, the man who still haunted her dreams. Sebastian couldn't believe his eyes. Hanna was there, smiling at him. She wanted to be with him. Elated, he smiled back down at her. She looked beautiful, radiant.

'Sebastian.' Hanna savoured the sound and the feel of the name that was so precious to her.

'Hanna.' Sebastian mimicked her. 'Haannna,' he tried again, attempting to pronounce the name in the proper Finnish fashion. This brought a giggle from Hanna, and Sebastian said it again, just to hear that sound again. He wasn't disappointed.

'Haaannna, shall we go somewhere to talk?'

'Yes, Sebastian.' She loved to say his name.

'My hotel is just around the corner – shall we go there?'

'Yes, Sebastian.' She had been saying "no" to him for far too long. 'But one more thing before we go.'

'Yes, my love?'

'That's exactly it.' Hanna took a deep breath, getting ready. 'I love you.'